BOOK 2 IN THE **DECEPTION** SERIES

DEEPER IN THE VEIL

NUCLEAR SECRETS. DEADLY GLOBAL GAMES.

ASIRA LELE

INDIA • SINGAPORE • MALAYSIA

Dedication

This book is dedicated to:

All those scientists (scientific and non-scientific) across India who have made pathbreaking strides in STEM, other fields of research, and medicine,

All those R&AW officers, IB officers, and agents who have assisted, protected, and spied for the Indian nuclear and space programs,

My dear late grandmother – Dr. Mrunalini (Meena) Joshi-Shirwadkar (d. Jan 2022), whose wisdom, accomplishments, and life are a marvel to all those who knew her,

And lastly, it is dedicated to you, my dear reader, for loving and caring for Bharat – our ever-giving homeland and Mother.

CONTENTS

CONTENTS

AUTHOR'S NOTE

From the year 2009 onwards, there were many unusual deaths of Indian nuclear scientists ranging from core research areas to the defence sector. The first killing was of Dr. Homi Bhabha in 1966. Many scientists linked with missile technology were also killed. These deaths happened in a seemingly unexplained, yet oddly systematic manner. Post-mortems were not even conducted in quite a few cases, and despite filing RTI applications and PILs in the High Court in 2015, there has been no substantial investigation into these deaths. Largely, the deaths have still remained as a subject for speculation for the Indian public. Out of respect, I have changed the names of the scientists who died. Senior voices of authority have pointed to the involvement of foreign intelligence agencies in the killings of these scientists. Foreign interests have always tried to thwart India's nuclear and missile technology progress in many covert ways.

While corruption and infighting exist at every level of our esteemed institutions; right from the police, judiciary, politics, defence, and nuclear research organisations, there are plenty of hidden venomous snakes who are poised to strike at any possible opportunity. However, it is up to every Indian not to feed these snakes or let them gain advantage to conduct nefarious activities that may dearly cost us our country. I know quite a few people who have unearthed such snakes and dragged them to the Prime Minister's Office. I salute the tenacity and mental strength of such folks who counter external spies as well as internal enemies.

While the situation is getting better, the journey towards an idyllic state of defence needs time. We have miles to go and all questions may not always have the answers we seek. India has evolved from the 1970s, and today in 2025, we nurture a certain culture of nuclear security. Any compromise on this issue must be dealt with at the highest levels.

Many folks are jointly working towards a better tomorrow. May those good and brave people in the shadows who protect us always remain blessed. There are such hidden gems planted everywhere on this soil and beyond its borders. May they protect the people of this beautifully diverse, secular nation and achieve all of India's geopolitical targets set for this century.

My sincere thanks to all those who contributed to this book – intelligence officers, editors, scientists, and my loving family.

Thank you!

The first face is what you show to the world.

The second face is what you show to your close friends and family.

The third face is what you never show anyone. And that is the truest reflection of who you are.

PROLOGUE

The sniper aimed the rifle carefully at his target.

Several feet below, Alisha Nair sprinted in the crowded streets of Palestine, beads of sweat dripping down her tanned neck. She glanced back in fear, knowing she was right in his crosshairs. *She's far too perceptive*, he thought. The sniper took a deep breath and calmed his mind. *Snipers are just like photographers*, he mused quizzically. *Both shoot people in similar yet different ways.* As he fingered the trigger, he steadied his heartbeat and pulse.

Alisha had just taken refuge behind an enormous basket of oranges in a fruit market. Barely breathing, the sniper watched the ripple of her black dress fade away from his glassy scope. *You can't hide from me.* He was almost amused. *I could wait all day.* The tall figure in black finally stepped out from behind the fruit basket, hurrying away. The crowd around her dispersed in a manner oddly convenient for him. *I've got her now,* he thought triumphantly.

In that infinitesimal second between two heartbeats, when the air froze in his nasal tracts, the sniper pulled the trigger. His target fell like a cast-out mannequin, blood spilling on the footpath. A little girl screamed, and the crowd's attention was rivetted on the fallen figure. A man barrelled out of nowhere screaming, "*Naziha…*" The sniper froze.

This target was wrong, utterly wrong.

Cursing himself, he frantically watched through his scope again. And then, he noticed a tall figure in a navy-blue Burqa climbing out from the *other* side of the fruit stall. He desperately grabbed his rifle again, but he knew it was too late. With a rear glance that seemed to look straight into his crosshairs, Alisha Nair plunged through the crowd, her feet slipping on the cobbled streets of Palestine.

She had just bought herself some time to survive.

As she sprinted, Alisha wondered if the nuclear threat had been stopped.

CHAPTER 1

May 2011 - Mumbai

There was nothing about the day to suggest anything sinister. And yet, the shadows of a silent and terrible fate had already crept around the corner.

In the radiation and photochemistry section of the Bhabha Atomic Research Centre (BARC), two brilliant young research scholars, Arjun Vasu and Pratik Bajaj, did not seem to notice the summer sun blazing outside their high-security facility. They were among the most promising minds in a team of chemical experts.

Pratik frowned as he glanced at Arjun's hand. "What's that?" he asked, pointing to a burn mark. Arjun shrugged, "You remember I told you about that fire in the lab last week? I got a minor burn from that." Pratik stared at it and said quietly, "You should have reported that. The BARC must be informed about such hazardous incidents in a high-security zone, especially when our lab is just a kilometre away from the nuclear reactors." Arjun shook his head, trying to concentrate on his work, "These things are a part of life when you work in a lab, Pratik. It wasn't a major fire, so I didn't report it. Lucky escape, you know."

Pratik began to reply but stopped when a familiar hissing sound caught his attention. Both scientists turned towards the noise and their expressions froze when they saw flames erupting across the lab. The fire spread rapidly, consuming the lab equipment in its wake. Panic surged through them as Arjun grabbed the door and pulled it, but it was jammed. He screamed, "Pratik help me, I can't open it." Together, they pulled at the door with all their might, but it didn't budge. The smoke thickened around them as Arjun finally fainted and collapsed to the floor. Pratik shuddered and felt his lungs choking in the thick, black smoke. *Where is the fire brigade?* He thought, dazed as he sank to the floor, trying to crawl away from the growing inferno.

An hour later, the police and firefighters stared in horror at the charred black remains of what used to be Arjun Vasu and Pratik Bajaj. The once merry, promising, and brilliant young research scholars from the group of chemical experts now lay charred beyond recognition, still crouched, inches away from the door.

* * *

A week later, Lalith Gopalan stared at the news article titled, *'Blaze at BARC kills two scientists'* as he sat in his office. Gopalan was a senior nuclear scientist at the Kaiga Atomic Power Station in Karnataka's quaint town of Kaiga near Karwar. He had known Arjun and Pratik from before. *They were good boys, with such bright and promising futures*, thought Gopalan with anguish. Unable to concentrate anymore, he decided to wrap up his day early. With a heavy heart, he started walking back home. Gopalan reminisced about the days when those young, eager boys had worked with him. He sighed and took a long sip from his water bottle.

Ever since a water cooler at his workplace was found laced with tritium, he preferred carrying water from home. More than fifty workers at Kaiga's nuclear power plant had fallen sick from the contamination. The investigation was still going on and the miscreants had not been found yet. Only today, Gopalan was chatting with a friendly police officer who had told him under strict confidence, that the tritium had come from Kaiga's own plant, and not brought in externally as they'd previously thought.

Gopalan's feet came to a sudden halt and his eyes widened with realisation. *The tritium came from our plant... but our tritium is kept under high security, where access is limited to only-*

Something heavy smashed into the back of his head and Gopalan cried out as he staggered forward. As his hands instinctively flew up to protect his face, he felt a powerful hand slam into his neck, dragging him into the thicket of trees lining the road next to him. His water bottle slipped from his numb fingers and rolled away into the mud. Gopalan choked out, but his cry for help went unheard on the desolate road.

Two days later, the bodies of Lalith Gopalan and another scientist, Naveen Mulay, were both found dead in the Kalindi River.

* * *

Dr. Uma Rangarajan winced as the doctor finished examining her knee. "Well, Dr. Rangarajan! You're in perfectly good shape." He said with a warm smile. Uma tucked a strand of silvery grey hair behind her ear. "So, what would you prescribe?" she asked. The doctor chuckled, "Nothing at all - no pills, no antibiotics. Just go home, oil your knees well, and skip this week's charity marathon. You'll be fine, your knee needs rest, that's all." Uma smiled and nodded. The doctor added, "You know, you inspire me, Dr. Rangarajan. I can only hope to have your energy and optimism at your age. I'm terribly grumpy quite often, even though I'm just touching thirty." Uma chuckled softly, "You remind me of my son. He's coming back home from America next month. It's been a while since I've seen him. Thank you, dear and all the best," she said, patting the doctor gently on the shoulder. As Uma limped out of the doctor's cabin, her eyes fell upon her picture prominently featured on the cover page of this month's science magazine which was popular in several national scientific organisations. She merely smiled and shook her head as she recalled the words of the young doctor. *Go home and take rest!* scoffed Uma. *Really, these young folks…*

Dr. Uma Rangarajan cherished her work at the Indira Gandhi Centre for Atomic Research (IGCAR) in Kalpakkam, near Chennai, in the state of Tamil Nadu. She was the head of the Women Scientists' Association as well, and was often invited to conduct lectures on nuclear physics in science colleges across the country. Dr. Uma Rangarajan had a passionate ambition to encourage more girls to pursue nuclear, defence, and space research in India. She mused, *Women have the potential to view and change the world in ways that men never can. They just need a chance.*

As she headed back to her lab, two familiar faces waited eagerly in her office. "Got the project approval, I see?" Uma said crisply. Dr. Iyer and S. Ananth beamed at her. "Come on, ma'am. We've waited so long for this missile project. We'll be working with the DRDO, too. We can't wait to start working on this with you next week." Uma settled in her chair and said, "Fine. Biryani at my place tonight, boys. It's the weekend anyway. I'll also make my special kheer for you. You deserve it." Dr. Iyer and Ananth cheered, their excitement echoing down the corridor.

On Monday morning, Dr. Uma Rangarajan was found dead in her home, having seemingly committed suicide. A bottle of sleeping pills was found next to her lifeless body. When the police rushed to Dr. Iyer's house, they found him hanging from his ceiling fan. S. Ananth had gone missing. Two days later, Ananth was found dead on a railway track in Chennai.

* * *

Somewhere in a dark room, the assassin stood tall on the cold stone floor. A smile of quiet satisfaction settled on the assassin's cherubic face. *I have a very unique skill set.* The cold seeped in through his thick layer of clothing, but the assassin hardly noticed. A gloved hand reached out to open a chest of drawers that hid a secret drawer. The assassin carefully dropped a sealed zip lock bag inside and turned away with a sadistic smirk.

He mused, *I bagged yet another prize.*

***

In the heartland of Mumbai, a tall man lounged in a black leather chair. He was known mysteriously as '*Knight*'. His sleek insurance office was discreet but exquisitely decorated. It had an air of sophistication, which subtly indicated that he dealt only with immensely wealthy clients. To his clients and the smartly dressed receptionist, Knight's identity had remained something of a mystery. He met his clients only through appointments. If anyone inquired about his identity, they were met with a cool, piercing, and intimidating gaze from under his external charm. He would merely repeat with a small smile, "Just call me Knight."

Knight's fingers lingered hesitatingly on the receiver of his desk phone. He wondered, *should I make the call now, or later?* Through the secure line, he dialled a number known only to him.

After the call connected, Knight spoke softly, "It's done."

***

Somewhere in China, a woman called Zheng Qui walked briskly down the footpath. Her black heels neatly crunched the fallen leaves under her quick steps. A gentle ringtone interrupted the evening calm, its melodic chime blending seamlessly into the air around her. Reaching into the pocket of her long beige coat, she pulled out a small cellphone and held it to her ear. The voice on the other end spoke only two terse words, "Beijing, *now.*" Her mouth curled in slight annoyance. *She'd just finished a mission only last week…*

With a deep breath, Zheng turned sharply and headed off in the opposite direction. She was part of the Yunnan State Security Department (YSSD), a branch of the Ministry of State Security (MSS), China's formidable intelligence agency. Zheng paused for a brief moment and gazed at the setting sun casting dancing spots of light and shadow on the marble steps in front of her. *We are the lethal shadows of the dark*, she thought as her black heels clicked rhythmically against the stone before she disappeared around the next corner.

✻ ✻ ✻

A few months earlier…

The Prime Minister of India tapped his pen impatiently against the thick, wooden conference table, the sound echoing faintly in the quiet room. For a moment, his eyes lingered on the Defence Minister's brooding expression that reflected on the table's polished teakwood surface. *This man is someone who could be trusted*, mused the Prime Minister. He was attending a closed-door meeting with very important dignitaries. Seated around the table were the Defence Minister, Home Minister, the Directors of the Defence Research and Development Organisation (DRDO) and Department of Atomic Energy (DAE), the Chief of Defence Staff, the Joint Secretary of the R&AW, and the National Security Advisor.

Defence Minister, Surya was a rather fiery man. He was not quite an elegant fit in Delhi's marble halls and the elite political class. However, the Prime Minister liked him for his no-nonsense attitude on national security. Surya was a man well into his fifties. Unlike other ministers in the cabinet, he had served in the territorial army, worked tirelessly for impoverished people at the ground level, and had spent several weeks with soldiers at the perilous Siachen Glacier. *A man who could get the job done.*

The Prime Minister returned his attention to Surya's words. "... India is the world's second-largest defence importer after Saudi Arabia. We make up 9.2% of the global arms import. We produce up to 50% of defence products that we use, and the rest is imported." Surya then addressed the Prime Minister directly, "Sir, we need to start producing defence equipment on a mass scale. Our brand of 'Made In India' would also ensure more jobs, and growth, and will boost India's GDP." The Director of DRDO said thoughtfully, "For this, we need to collaborate more with the private sector and research institutes. We need to start relying on IITs and other such institutes, instead of relying only on the government's industries."

The Chief of Defence Staff said wearily, "It's not that simple. There are plenty of arms dealers and agents within the defence sector. Their involvement is critical for any defence deal to take place between foreign defence companies and the Indian Government. In fact, arms agents can manipulate the procurement process because they have the means to pay substantial commissions to politicians, military officials, and bureaucrats. That is why they're usually present in defence deals. I know cases where arms agents have even manipulated reports of weapons tests. These agents even have access to classified intelligence and they're all too familiar with the inner workings of our defence ministry. It is difficult to weed them out."

The National Security Advisor glanced at the Prime Minister and said quietly, "Sir, long ago we moved our attention from Pakistan to China. But we need to put it out there in bold and make India's presence acutely felt as a global counter-threat to China's aggression. In the South Asian region, we are their main challenge. If China attacks us again, then we need to be prepared – lock, stock, and barrel."

The Home Minister unexpectedly began, "Well, I don't think China would-" But Defence Minister, Surya cut him off sharply. "Would attack us in today's times, *Ji*? *WOULD*?" spat Surya who was normally on good terms with the Home Minister. "And what then, stupidly say '*Hindi-Chini Bhai Bhai*' like Nehru, even when those Chinese bastards were at our doorsteps, slaughtering our soldiers? Or be a blundering fool like Morarji Desai and shut down our Research and Analysis Wing?" The Home Minister lowered his gaze.

Surya looked at the National Security Advisor and asked, "What is on *your* mind, sir?"

The shrewd man merely smiled and said quietly, "We need to increase our *Shakti* in the aggressive language that China and America understand better. *Anushakti*. It is a path that we have already taken long ago. Do you remember Project Devil? In 1973 our then-Prime Minister, Indira Gandhi unofficially launched and funded a secret project called Project Devil. Project Devil was one of two early liquid-fueled missile projects that India developed, along with Project Valiant. The goal of Project Devil was to produce a short-range surface-to-surface missile. Although discontinued in 1980 without achieving full success, Project Devil led to the later development of the Prithvi missile in the 1980s.

Even today, we need to expand those missions ahead. An excellent example is our own missiles technology base on the Dr. APJ Abdul Kalam Island near Orissa. We need to establish India as a nuclear power in as many sectors of defence as possible, and especially counter the ports in South Asia that China has seized. Nuclear submarines can be deployed in those areas where China sends its ships to spy on India. Many countries in South Asia have leased their base to China as military ports. The most recent example of this is the 99-year lease of the Hambantota International Port in Sri Lanka to China.

Going ahead, we need more young Indians in nuclear engineering for many purposes, not just defence. China had created 'Program 863' in the 1980s. This program was specially created to stimulate the development of advanced technologies in a wide range of fields that would make China independent of financial obligations to foreign technologies. We need to create something similar for India."

The Prime Minister turned to the Director of the Department of Atomic Energy and asked briefly, "How much time do you require to introduce new projects in our nuclear institutions?" The Director replied confidently, "With your blessing, it would hardly take a few weeks, sir." The Prime Minister nodded slowly in satisfaction. *There is always so much to plan... and so little time.* "Thank you, gentlemen." After the meeting was adjourned, one by one, the dignitaries rose with their hands folded in a respectful *Namaskar* and left the room. Defence Minister, Surya, the Joint Secretary of the R&AW, and the National Security Advisor, however, stayed back. After the other dignitaries were out of earshot, the Prime Minister turned to the men who were still in the room, and spoke urgently, "Now, tell me *your* plans."

The National Security Advisor pulled out a file from his bag and placed it on the table. He leant forward and began, "Sir, it is my firm opinion that we need to put out a range of our K-Family missiles. Thanks to Dr. Kalam, our K-4 and K-5 missiles are enough to protect us or launch a counter-attack in the land or sea. The DRDO developed the K-4 version as a nuclear-capable, intermediate-range submarine-launched ballistic missile to arm the Arihant-class submarines. This missile's maximum range is about 3500 kilometres. Our Sagarika missile, also known by the code names K-15 or B-05 has a range of 750 kilometres. It was designed for retaliatory nuclear strikes and is an important part of India's nuclear triad." The Prime Minister gave a nod of understanding as Surya listened with rapt attention.

The Advisor continued, "Sir, we understand and strictly abide by our no-first nuclear policy. Our neighbouring countries however understand the nuclear threat as the most formidable one, even though there are plenty of other ways to issue a threat, especially through finance and trade. Considering China as a direct threat to our national security more than Pakistan, we need to strengthen all aspects of our nuclear research program, irrespective of the government in power. Nobody would be able to match China in cyber warfare. It is, therefore, my opinion that we conduct this program as 'Operation Anushakti', a long-term plan for India's nuclear welfare.

Let us invest by gathering our bright minds and upgrading the levels of our nuclear research at all institutes, regardless of whether we use it for defence, offence, or as a source of energy. The missiles will of course be used for military strength. The by-products of that research could also be exported to international markets. And we need to slowly start lessening the volume of imports wherever possible, sir. We can surely create high-quality materials locally, at much lower costs.

That way, we wouldn't need to worry about America slapping nuclear sanctions on us at any point in time. Of course, considering the vast array of materials that nuclear power requires, we still need foreign collaborations to develop and implement that research. But going ahead, we need to start reducing dependencies." A silence of contemplation fell upon the room after his long speech.

The Prime Minister turned to Surya and asked, "And what is your opinion on this, Surya *Ji*?" Surya nodded and chuckled, "Well, local produce is going to anger the international community, especially France and America. We have a lot of nuclear material imports from across various countries that cost us millions. If we do this, then we need to expect arm-twisting in foreign markets for losing their capital." Surya shrugged and added bluntly, "And I'm prepared to deal with them."

He scribbled a few notes in his notebook and continued, "We would require a few more meetings with the respective chiefs of research institutions. As this would be a highly classified and sensitive program, we need to involve agents from the R&AW and the IB besides our army intelligence wing, to keep eyes and ears out everywhere and report how the winds are changing in our direction for this operation. At a later point when things take up speed, we would also need to keep some of them across the country on standby to neutralise anything or anyone that may obstruct this operation. I will arrange for a meeting with both the national security directors this week. This is going to be an operation for a long-term profit for India." The Joint Secretary of the R&AW bowed his head with approval.

The Prime Minister gave Surya a satisfied nod and said quietly to all of them, "I am giving you all the official go-ahead for Operation *Anushakti*. Good luck and Jai Hind."

Present Day, India

Alisha Nair grit her teeth as she was slammed to the ground yet again. Panting, she glared up at her godfather and mentor, Ravi Pathak, who was now grinning down at her. She tried to roll over, but he'd locked her in a powerful chokehold that even she, a seasoned fighter, couldn't break. "Think!" he said smiling at her with infuriating encouragement. Alisha grasped his forearms and pulled him down, but he'd already anticipated her counterattack. It was a very well-matched combat, but after a long struggle, Alisha finally gave up. She lay on her back for a while, fuming at herself. "Oh, please. Get up," chuckled Pathak. She sat up cross-legged on the floor, brushed her hair out of her eyes, and continued to glare at Pathak.

"You're still like an open book in hand-to-hand combat, Alisha. I can read you *that* easily," said Ravi Pathak, pulling off his combat arm sleeves, soaked with sweat. "If *I* can anticipate your moves, then the enemy would have already studied you before attacking you lethally. That's enough training for today." Alisha sprang to her feet and stretched. They had been practicing combat fighting at home today. Her husband, Raghav Nair was due any moment from work. "Uncle Ravi, aren't you staying for dinner?" she asked, frowning as Pathak headed for the door. "I'll drop in tomorrow my dear," he replied, giving her an affectionate kiss on her forehead. "I have a few reports coming in at the bureau early tomorrow morning. Tell Raghav, I said hi."

As Ravi Pathak left, Alisha's eyes followed him. A quiet mix of warmth and fondness, tinged with the anxiety that a daughter feels for her father rose in her throat. Alisha loved and cared deeply for her godfather. Her eyes glazed over as she recalled her last, dangerous mission not too long ago.

She could never forget Uncle Ravi's face, contorted in pure rage when she'd been shot at by an ISI agent, Jamaal Khan. The bullet had only grazed her, and even though she had healed, she could still feel that burning sensation against her skin as if it had happened only yesterday. *How many lives had we saved together during that mission?* Alisha bowed her head in gratitude at the father figure that the fates had bestowed upon her after she'd lost her parents. *The parents I lost, and the family I received.*

Sometimes, Alisha missed having a motherly touch in her life, but she'd refused to give in to that crushing sadness. Uncle Ravi had made up for the absence of both her parents and had trained Alisha hard enough to get through everything that life threw at her. Her fingers trailed lightly over the scar that the bullet had left. She felt grateful to be a part of an organisation that countered terror attacks. It was grueling work, both mentally and physically. But Alisha wouldn't have it any other way. *Fewer families would be broken apart*, she thought.

Her reverie was interrupted by the sound of Raghav Nair's car pulling up in the driveway. Alisha peeked through the curtain with a welcoming smile. Her eyes softened as she recalled how Raghav had taken care of her when she'd finally returned home, battered and bruised from her mission. Raghav had never asked or prodded her for answers. And yet, Alisha was almost sure that Raghav had somehow known everything already. *But how?* He had never given the slightest indication of it.

However, much later, she had opened up to him at last. Her floodgates had burst, and she told him of the secrets that she'd guarded for more than two decades. He had listened to her, with tears in his eyes. Alisha could never forget that night. Raghav had only stared at the ceiling without uttering a single word and had wrapped his arms tightly around her in bed, locking her to his chest. They were now back to their space of warm comfort and love where they could freely share anything, without any misunderstandings.

And yet, when Alisha stared every night at the mysterious gold bracelet that Raghav had gifted her, curiosity gnawed at her. The bracelet glinted on her wrist in the dark. The powerful words, 'धर्मो रक्षति रक्षितः' or 'Dharmo Rakshati Rakshitah:' that were inscribed on its inside seemed to reach out to her. 'Dharma protects those who uphold it.'

She knew her husband better than anyone else, and yet sometimes she couldn't shake off the feeling - *Who was Raghav Nair?* He was perfect on paper, and yet even now, after all these years, she'd felt that something did not add up. She thought to herself, *or maybe, I'm just being stupid. Learn to trust your husband, you idiot,* she shook her head to dismiss the thoughts.

Her muddled thoughts were interrupted as the front door opened. As he walked in, Raghav's eyes met Alisha's, and a tender smile crossed his face. She grinned at him as she pulled off his work bag from his shoulders. "Long day?" she asked, giving him a quick hug despite his sweat-drenched blue shirt. He kissed her nose lightly and murmured, "Let me shower first." Alisha chuckled, her grin widening, "Go ahead. I'm joining you." Raghav's face lit up, "See you in there, sweetheart," he said with a delighted grin.

Alisha took her time. She undid her long hair and let it fall down her back as she headed up the staircase. She could hear the sound of the water gushing in the bathroom. She undressed herself and tossed her clothes on the bed. As she opened the bathroom, a cloud of steam surrounded her.

She paused for a moment, gazing at Raghav, who stood still with his eyes closed under the hot shower. *This guy really enjoys a hot shower,* she thought, smiling. Alisha walked up to him and wrapped her arms around his neck, allowing the hot water to run through her hair. Raghav turned around, put his hands around her waist, and pulled her close. His warm chest pressed into her soft, wet breasts. Drops of hot water clung to her nipples. His hand moved into Alisha's dark, soaking hair as he hungrily pulled her into a deep kiss. His lips moved to her throat and bit her gently, licking off the water from the nape of her neck. She shivered with pleasure and kissed him back. "Hold still," she smirked. Her lips moved down his chest slowly and seductively, all the while kissing his wet skin. "Well, hello there…" teased Alisha, grasping his aroused shaft. He gasped as she put it in her mouth and sucked. He threw his head back, moaning, clutching her hair as she sucked him with a torrid passion.

After Alisha finally fell back, Raghav hauled her to her feet and whispered, "My turn." His tongue curled against her nipples, gently biting, and sucking the moisture from her wet skin. He slowly made his way down, smirked at her, and said, "Good luck handling this, darling." His warm tongue darted inside her soft, silky wetness. Alisha started trembling as he sucked her clit, thrusting his tongue deep into her, feeding on the warm wetness. She threw her head back and gave a soft scream of pleasure.

Raghav relaxed and straightened himself up. He grasped her slender waist and slammed her against the wall. His hands slowly crept up her legs, feeling the rivulets of hot water that ran down her skin. He hoisted her up and seized the top of her ear gently with his lips. Legs dangling in the air, Alisha moaned with carnal pleasure as he entered her slowly. Her nails raked against his wet skin, desperate for respite. He moved in a slow rhythm and closed his eyes, feeling every inch of her wetness against his shaft. Her fingers grasped his hair, and she begged him, "Harder." But he merely smirked at her, now moving in circles inside her. "Please," she implored him. Raghav grasped her hands and locked them above her head. He stared at her with lust and pushed his lips against hers, sucking on her tongue. As she fell back again, he bit his lips, gently thrusting into her.

Alisha bit into his shoulder and desire flooded through Raghav. He grasped her waist tightly and drove into her harder. She cried with pleasure, and he plunged deeper and faster. He felt her muscles tightening around him as she screamed in climax. He released himself just as he pulled out, dripping wet. Panting, he set her down and she fell into his arms. They rested against the wall, the hot water offering a soothingly sweet comfort.

Alisha finally turned off the tap. Hands still trembling, she reached for the towels. She wiped them both, as Raghav watched her lovingly, hands still wrapped around her waist. "Let's go out somewhere to eat," he whispered in her ear.

Later in the night, as they lay together, Raghav pulled an extra blanket over Alisha and lightly kissed her forehead. "Thank you," she murmured sleepily, pulling him close. Smiling, they slept peacefully, their arms wrapped around each other.

✳ ✳ ✳

In the Parliament Assembly, members raised questions about the recent unnatural deaths of the nuclear scientists. A member from the opposition party roared, "There has been an alarming increase in the deaths of our nuclear scientists. We also need to address the incident of the contaminated water cooler at Kaiga's nuclear plant. The fire incident at BARC has still not been resolved. Why has the government not said anything about the Kaiga culprits?"

A member from the ruling party stood up and responded, "We are investigating these incidents on a high-priority basis. This government in power takes national security seriously, unlike your party that was in power last time." His words were met with an uproar.

Meanwhile, the common citizens of India merely shook their heads at their television screens and changed the channel. Like always, they were anyway bound to forget about these incidents after a couple of weeks.

* * *

It was a typical morning for Officer Ravindra Pathak at the Intelligence Bureau in Pune. His desk was neatly organized with a stack of reports and files, each one carefully tied up with white string, awaiting his attention. However, he reached to pick up a steaming cup of his favourite cardamom *chai* in front of him. *An Indian's day cannot start without chai,* he thought staring at his reports. *Or coffee, for that matter,* he chuckled to himself.

As he sat back in his chair, Pathak thought about his last mission with Alisha. *A close encounter,* he thought as his eyebrows knit together. He'd written the mission report all by himself and had drafted it very carefully. One confidential, sealed copy now lay in the Intelligence Bureau's archives, while the other copies had been sent to Delhi. Discreet action had been taken by his team, and a few more arrests had been made in the case. An ISI officer, Jamaal Khan had been eliminated. A major drug supply racket had been busted. Those drugs had been circulated in India and its profits were used as funds for creating terrorist activities in India. A famous politician had been ruined. Pathak smiled faintly. He'd have to find a way to silence that bastard forever. *Politicians like Prasad Thakur need to be permanently buried,* he thought viciously.

Pathak drained his *chai* and started reading his reports. As he pulled out the third file, a note lay on top of the next one. *Why was it hidden like this?* He wondered. Frowning, Pathak picked it up and unfolded it. It contained only a few words in purple letters:

'*Jaguar - Two weeks. Prepare.*'

Pathak froze and stared at the note. He had not been referred to as Jaguar for several years. A sudden feeling of apprehension built in his stomach as he realised who had sent it.

Delhi was calling.

CHAPTER 2

Tel Aviv, Israel

In Tel Aviv, Israel, the sky was overcast. Grey clouds loomed over the tall buildings. A small group of children stared anxiously at the skies, wondering if they would still be able to play. A bright yellow ball lay forgotten at their feet on the playground. "It looks like it's going to rain any minute now," said little Shira anxiously. No sooner had she spoken that the rain began to pour.

As the children pushed each other to run home from the playground, little Shira reached down to collect the wet ball. When she straightened up again, she noticed a man with distinct light-golden hair watching her from a window in the building across the playground. A sudden roar of thunder startled her, and Shira staggered back. She glanced up at the window again and blinked in confusion.

The golden-haired man had vanished.

***

At the Mossad headquarters in Tel Aviv, the head of the Iranian desk, Katriel Levy, pored over the latest reports that had just come in from the Sayeret Matkal. The Sayeret Matkal was one of the main field intelligence-gathering units of Israel that conducted deep reconnaissance behind enemy lines to obtain strategic intelligence. Katriel drummed her fingers on the table as she finished reading the reports. Brows knitted together, she stared at the beige walls of her office, lost in thought.

With pursed lips, she reached for the secure line of her desk phone and spoke only one instruction, with a steady voice of authority, "Get me *Raphael.*" As she placed the receiver back, a tense smile crossed her face, "*This should be interesting...*" she murmured.

* * *

Ben Shapiro strode down the long corridor, his jacket slung carelessly over his lean shoulders. The fading light from the pouring grey clouds cast a dark tinge on his light golden hair. He thought about the group of children playing with the yellow ball before the rain started. *Such innocence,* he smiled to himself. He was engrossed in watching them play from a distant window before he received a call to report to duty. *Really, how humans change when they grow up*, he wondered.

As Ben stepped into the elevator, heading toward the Iranian desk, his blue eyes lingered on the enormous Mossad logo etched into the grey wall several floors below. The Mossad was short for *HaMossad leModi'in uleTafkidim Meyuhadim*, which translated to 'The Institute for Intelligence and Special Operations'. Ben, however, liked to call it '*Ha'Midrasha*' or 'The Institute'. He cast an amused eye at the changed motto of the Mossad. Previously, it was '*With wise guidance, you can wage your war.*' But now, it had changed to, '*Where there is no wise direction, the nation falls; but in the multitude of counsellors, there is safety.*' Ben had been summoned by Katriel Levy, the head of the Iran desk. *There's my wise direction and counselling*, chuckled Ben to himself as he knocked on Katriel's door.

"*Shalom*, Kaf," he greeted her. It had been so many years to her nickname, that he'd forgotten who had picked it for her. She nodded at him with her brows furrowed, and merely said, "Raphael." He looked at her in mild surprise. Normally, Katriel addressed him with an array of colorful, often profane names. They had graduated together and had remained close friends even at Ha'Midrasha and had even served in Lebanon together. "Okay, this is serious," frowned Ben, noting the authoritative tone in her voice. "What did I do now?" Katriel sighed and ran her fingers through her brown curls. "Sayeret Matkal has reported a new development in Iran. Shin Bet has confirmed it as well."

Ben looked at her evenly and shrugged his shoulders as he spoke, "Nothing we haven't handled before." Katriel shook her head slightly. "We have received information that Iran is building another nuclear power plant. This time, however, it is way underground and fortified." Ben's blue eyes fixed on her in a thoughtful gaze, and his brows furrowed slightly. He spoke, "I still don't see how that's a problem." Katriel nodded at him and said, "We need to take it down *before* it becomes a problem. I'm sending a file to the Prime Minister tomorrow." Ben scratched his chin, processing the information. "Fine. Get me your reports on this. I'll draw up a plan and decide the teams."

Katriel said tersely, "Leave everything else and focus only on this as of now. Knowing the Prime Minister, he's going to arrange a meeting with our director right away. Pick your teams carefully, Ben. This isn't going to be an easy operation."

Ben smiled faintly at her and murmured, "It never is."

* * *

Meanwhile, in Mumbai, rare earth elements expert Jayesh Rao whistled as he brewed his special tea. His wife had already prepared his favourite Sunday breakfast - *pohe*, sprinkled lightly with lemon juice and coriander. "Don't eat all the *pohe* Jayesh," she warned him, laying out two bowls on the table before stepping out to purchase groceries. He had just finished reading the newspaper and was feeling utterly at peace in his khaki shorts. He was expecting a visitor to arrive soon. It was a journalist who was working on a college report on India's rare earth elements and wanted an expert's opinion. Jayesh wanted to guide such young folks in the future. He was looking forward to a retired life. He'd served well in the Indian Rare Earths Limited government corporation.

The bell rang and Jayesh opened the door, beaming. He seated his cherub-faced, smiling visitor and placed two bowls of hot *pohe* on the small table. "I'll just bring the tea," said Jayesh cheerfully, jerking his head towards the kitchen.

Half an hour later when Jayesh's wife came back, her arms laden with grocery bags, she was slightly puzzled to see the door ajar. As she walked into the living room, her bag of apples slipped from her numb hands. She screamed until her neighbours rushed into the house. They found Jayesh Rao slumped lifeless across the sofa with his glasses askew, with his legs spilling over the floor.

* * *

The man known as 'Knight' leaned forward to pick up his ringing phone. A voice on the other end spoke only one word very softly, "*Eight.*"

Knight replied, "That'll be enough for now. Wait for my instructions." He hung up the phone. He did not like wasting time on foot soldiers. *They weren't the ones building an empire like he was. Ethics did not have a place in his empire.* He glanced up from his desk to see his staff working diligently in their cubicles. He could watch them through a narrow glass pane in his enormous cabin. However, they couldn't see him. Knight had designed it in a way that nobody could watch from the outside what he was doing.

Knight's cell phone buzzed. The screen displayed an incoming payment of 3000 dollars. *That would do*, he smirked, *for now*. Knight already co-owned a finance start-up in Qatar, and it was thriving. He pooled his money strategically, diverting it to expand his portfolio. Knight was the man whom wealthy folks turned to for dark favours. *The rich did not like to get their own hands dirty. They preferred to outsource these tasks*, thought Knight in cold amusement. He had ordered a model tonight for his pleasure. She would be shared later by a prominent politician, but Knight couldn't care less. The more exciting prospect was a new deal that he was expecting.

And that deal was going to be the pleasure of his lifetime.

✳ ✳ ✳

Raghav Nair sat in his office, drafting plans for the next month. Earlier in the day, he had finished two important business meetings. Now, he had just finished briefing his employees on the upcoming month's targets. Diversifying and expanding business portfolios was always a roller-coaster ride, but Raghav sailed through it with cool, ruthless precision. And he enjoyed every single minute of it. Raghav mentally thanked his grandfather, *Nana*, for his sharp business acumen. Nair Ventures was growing more than ever, and Raghav planned how he was going to shape it in the direction he wanted it to grow. His total employee strength was steadily increasing and the senior ones rarely left. To him, this was a good sign. He was pleased with the company's turnover in the last quarter.

He was slowly focusing more and more on government infrastructure contracts. These were projects that yielded handsome long-term benefits, but Raghav hated the bureaucracy and bribery that came along with it.

His gaze fell on the photo frame of his parents. *You would've been proud of your son, you know*, he told his parents silently. *You would've been proud of the boy you raised.* He sighed, knowing that his inner voice would never reach them. Raghav suddenly missed them. *And you would've loved her*, he thought wistfully, looking at Alisha's frame on his desk.

His brows furrowed as he stared at his wife's photo. *Can she truly deal with her line of work?* Alisha had told him of her profession. Their marriage had healed. In fact, it was better than ever, and they were living their dream. But Raghav had been silent about it. Alisha was more capable than almost anyone he'd known. Even though he trusted her completely, there were always human limitations. Raghav knew what it took to make sacrifices, especially those for the nation. *I won't let anything happen to her,* thought Raghav with a feeling of finality. *She has suffered enough.*

Raghav glanced at his wristwatch and got up with a start. He'd nearly forgotten Alisha's reminder to leave the office early today for the party at their house. He quickly skimmed over his day's reports… *Everything looks fine for today.* He slung his bag over his shoulder and dashed off.

How does Alisha do it all, he wondered as his car sped home. They both despised parties and preferred the quiet peace of their home. The corner of Raghav's mouth turned downwards in a sardonic smile. He reflected on Alisha's words, *appearances needed to be kept.* But strangely, he was looking forward to co-hosting this party with her; something he had never felt before. He realised that since everything was much better between them, he looked forward to spending every minute with her. His life was no longer melancholy or mechanical when he was with her. They had come out stronger together in their healed marriage.

Raghav rushed inside the door and froze at the beautiful vision that stood smiling right in front of him. Alisha was dressed in a silver one-shoulder dress that split at her thigh. Silver and white diamond earrings glimmered through her hair which fell past her shoulders in soft waves. Raghav's mouth fell open, and she laughed as he stared at her from head to toe. He quickly closed it and stammered, "Well… wow." He was suddenly reminded of the day he'd first met her. She chuckled and replied, "Go upstairs, your suit is kept ready on the bed. The guests will arrive after half an hour, so get ready fast." "Yes ma'am", he replied, still staring at her. "Go," she urged and aimed a playful kick at him. He dodged her kick and sprinted upstairs, almost tripping over the first step as he was still ogling her. Alisha's laughter rang in his ears all the way upstairs.

An hour later, laughter and music filled their home as their guests helped themselves to drinks and elaborate savoury snacks. Alisha ensured that she catered to the needs of every single person in the group. And this time, to her surprise, Raghav joined, looking suave in the dark suit that she'd arranged for him. The large group was an interesting combination of artists from the film and music industry, wealthy business people, sportsmen and women, and a few people from the government who were close to the business fraternity. Alisha carefully noted whose eyes were drawn to whom. She could easily spot the beginning of an affair even before it already happened. She noted who was interested in whom and for what purpose. Raghav observed her keenly as she talked and laughed with the guests, cheerfully refilling their glasses, while mentally taking several notes. He smiled faintly, knowing that after the party she would most probably note down everything that took place and submit a covert report to someone in the higher circles of authority. He gave a rather blissful sigh, *perhaps these parties aren't all that bad.*

For a brief moment, Raghav's eyes met Alisha's. He smirked at her, but his gaze silently conveyed, *do what you're supposed to do, darling.* A quiet smile passed between them both, and only they seemed to perfectly understand what the other meant. As she turned back to the guests, a faint crease appeared between Raghav's eyebrows. His mind flew to his worried thoughts about her this afternoon, wondering if she could truly survive this line of work. He wished there was some way he could look out for her, even when she was away from him. *I cannot lose her.*

Raghav decided to arrange a meeting with a very old friend; a certain silver-haired gentleman with the codename, *'Dhruv'.*

✳ ✳ ✳

At the Intelligence Bureau, Ravi Pathak paced restlessly up and down in his office. He was waiting for a call from Delhi. He had already started to prepare his team and had marked out the right agents within and outside the IB, who could be called for a mission at a moment's notice.

Almost as if on cue, his secure desk phone rang. Pathak leapt to answer it eagerly. The voice on the other line only spoke, *"Jaguar."* Pathak froze. A wary expression crossed his face as he remembered that voice. *It had been what, twenty years?* A chilling memory of his younger past surfaced in his mind…

He stood ankle-deep in the watery slush, staring at the man whom he'd fatally stabbed. His fist was clenched tightly over the handle of a blood-soaked knife. Though it was a rather secluded area, his heart hammered as he prayed that nobody spotted him in such a sensitive area in the Dras Valley in Kashmir. Pathak glanced up at the grey skies and brushed off powdered snowflakes that had settled into his thick black woolen cowl. The white snow at his feet steadily turned murkier as drops of thick red blood dripped off the blade and mixed with the snowy slush. He had just killed the right-hand man of a dreaded terrorist. He'd been observing his prey for a long time. It had been a shrewdly calculated, quick, and clean kill, executed during a snowstorm when everybody was inside their homes.

Pathak glanced up at the house where his main target was holed up. Codenamed 'Ghalib', he was wanted for conducting several terror attacks across Kashmir and for the brutal murders of several Kashmiri Pandits. The curtains were drawn, and nobody had spotted Pathak. He reached down and dragged the body to an adjacent cottage. Luckily, that cottage had been the only safehouse within several kilometers. The door flew open, and a man helped him drag the body inside. This man had been a trusted asset for several years. Pathak hurried out in the howling wind and quickly removed the remaining evidence. The snowstorm would take care of the rest anyway. He quickly glanced up and down the street. He was numb and freezing, but he found himself thanking the weather. The snowstorm was a miracle that ensured all the locals were locked inside their homes today. He ran back to the cottage.

The man turned to Pathak and said, "You can't have Ghalib. Your backup isn't coming." Pathak stared at him, "What? But he's right there-" he jerked his thumb in the direction of the target's house. "I can finish him off in twenty minutes." The man shook his head sadly, "I just received higher orders." Pathak felt a slow rage boiling deep inside him. "Tell our captain that it is Ghalib, confirmed. I know how Ghalib moves and acts, I know it's him in that house. We can't have second thoughts right now when this is such a golden opportunity. If we don't kill him, then this situation will only get worse."

The man sighed, "I am ordered to physically prevent you from entering Ghalib's house for now, Jaguar. I'm sorry, but it is for your own safety as well. Now help me dispose of this body. This will take us some time and the snowstorm will hinder us a bit." Pathak felt like letting out a roar of frustration. How could they do this? If he just defied those orders right now, he could kill that bastard of a terrorist.

Without a second thought, he wrenched open the door, but a strong arm snaked around his chest, pulling him back into the house. The man begged him as Pathak tried to twist out of his grip, "Please, Jaguar..." The door slammed shut, and Pathak's fingers were still outstretched in futile desperation, trying to reach the target he was now ordered not to kill. Months of preparation had just gone to waste. He knew that Ghalib too, would take advantage of the snowstorm and would slip out of their clutches within a few crucial hours. As Pathak sagged and rested against the door, he was filled with terrible anguish, knowing that he had failed all those poor victims...

He was jolted from his reverie as the voice on the other line continued, "We have booked your flight to Delhi this week. A taxi will pick you up." The line cut off. Pathak replaced the phone slowly.

It had been more than twenty years. And yet, she had not changed.

CHAPTER 3

Beijing, China

Zheng Qui sat expectantly in front of her superior officer at the Indian desk. She'd just finished reading her mission's file. "You have everything you need in there," said the officer pointing to the file kept in front of her. "If you have any questions, call me on the phone given to you by the office. You will update me thrice a week about your operation. If you need any help, the MSS station chiefs in our target countries will help you."

The officer surveyed her for a moment and then continued, "Ensure discretion on the finance trails. I'll also give you some contacts in the Indian media. We've got some tips from an ISI asset as well. Every month, we need twenty articles against the current Indian government, and twenty-five articles encouraging Indians to buy more from companies owned by China. I want these articles published across multiple newspapers in English as well as in all their local languages. Also, spread Chinese cultural articles in Indian newspapers. We need to start disrupting India's most recent developments. The other agencies have already started the work long back." Zheng nodded. She slipped a notepad inside the file, on which she'd made elaborate points for herself. She liked everything neat – her cases, her desk, even her kills… *This mission was different than the previous ones,* she realised. *But this should be easy,* she thought to herself smugly.

She longed to go back to her previous work as a Chinese businessperson in Africa. *Why was she even dealing with India right now?* Zheng had bagged many government contracts across Africa that had paved the way for China securing more power at the United Nations. She even enjoyed Africa's raw beauty and its wildlife. The corner of her thin mouth turned downwards in slight disappointment. She was better as a desk analyst instead of being on the field. But it was prudent not to ask questions to her superiors. *There must be some reason why I'm put here for now*, she thought, walking down the corridor. Zheng shrugged but slowly smiled. She'd already finished mapping her mission's plans in her head. Her eyes caught a spider scuttling away from the windowsill.

Such an interesting species... Zheng could relate to spiders in so many ways – delicate yet deadly in their pursuit. Their webs, just like her plans, were as lethal as they were beautiful.

* * *

Delhi, India

Ravi Pathak stood in front of the R&AW headquarters in Delhi. He took a moment to soak in the feel of the nondescript white building. The warm Delhi sun bathed him as he closed his eyes, reminiscing the last time he was here. *It had been a long while ago.* He let out a small sigh and ran a tired hand through his greying hair. He adjusted his bag across his shoulders and trudged inside almost reluctantly. There were quite a few security layers to pass. *I'm definitely happier at the Intelligence Bureau*, he thought.

About twenty minutes later, Pathak sat in a somber-looking room. The glass door opened, and Pathak swivelled his chair to stand up. *There we go, now.*

"Hello Jaguar," said a voice, *the codename earned through sweat and blood.*

A short woman stood in front of him, offering a handshake. The corners of her mouth turned up slightly in a reluctant greeting. Pathak surveyed her and quipped, "You haven't changed, Radhika." She replied bluntly, "Yes, Pathak. Some people don't." Pathak smiled at her mockingly, taking in her appearance. Dressed in a simple *Salwar Khameez*, Radhika Menon was a stout little woman with short hair and glasses. At first glance, one would normally guess that she would most likely be an extremely strict Mathematics teacher with a perpetual frowning expression that suggested she was probably about to hit her students with her handbag or a ruler. Or she was probably a bored homemaker generally frustrated with her marriage or spouse.

Looking at Radhika Menon, one could never guess that she was one of R&AW's masterminds in strategising sensitive counter-terrorism operations and was well-versed in pattern analysis. Radhika Menon was deeply respected by the top brass in the Indian army who had worked with her closely on operations around the border areas.

Menon sat at the small table and indicated Pathak to sit directly in front of her. She started crisply, "Pathak, more than a month ago, our nuclear scientists started dying mysteriously from across several nuclear plants and institutions. I believe you must have already heard about it from the news." *It wasn't a question.* Pathak nodded. Menon looked straight at him. "I want you to investigate the death patterns and be the IB lead on this case." Pathak looked at her in surprise and raised his thick eyebrows. Menon continued in a low voice, "There is a program approved by the Prime Minister that will give India an impetus in the field of nuclear research.

Now, threats to nuclear scientists are usually divided into four areas based on their station and operation. The residential societies of our nuclear scientists are vulnerable pockets and possible target areas. The staff quarters are normally located inside the facility's premises, so they're well-guarded.

Even though we cannot prove it as of now, our guess is that the deaths of all these scientists are connected with this program. The problem is, we have very little evidence. The police are keen to close most of these cases as apparent suicides, and we need the Intelligence Bureau to take over. R&AW will provide you with any assistance you require." Pathak looked at her evenly and repeated, "*Any* assistance? Are you sure about that?"

Menon gave him a hard look and finally closed her eyes. "Pathak," she said sternly as she pinched the bridge of her nose in frustration, "This won't be another Kashmir. This time, I'm letting you take the complete lead. A successful operation can take place only if one learns from past mistakes." Pathak's hazel eyes hardened. "And will you be ready to comply with any information I need, this time?" Menon snapped, "About the case? Yes. Everything else is need-to-know." Pathak's temper flared slightly, "Like it was last time… in Kashmir?" Both stared at each other, nostrils flared, and jaws clenched.

Menon finally sighed. "Look Pathak, I chose you for this because of many reasons." Pathak's eyebrows shot up. She continued, "You and I have had our differences. But you're still one of the best goddamn IB officers I've worked with, who has a statistically proven, near-perfect instinct. I saw that in Kashmir. Years ago, I should've given you the go-ahead to kill Ghalib right there when you asked for it. That is the biggest regret of my career, and I'm owning up that mistake. I need more reliance on instincts here. You're as good at field operations as I am at analysis. In this case, I feel that there's something huge going on *because* there's systematically very less evidence in all deaths. We have a pattern of accidents. So, you and I need to put a special unit together to counter whoever is messing with our nuclear research. Your investigation reports will be read by the Prime Minister as well. I'll send all the relevant case documents to you at your office."

Pathak was quiet for a moment. "Fine. But I'm putting a condition, Menon." She looked at him questioningly. Pathak said grimly, "If or when I ask you to give me a go-ahead on something, then *don't stop me this time.*" Menon held up a hand and said, "I have obligations to answer to the-" But Pathak cut off, "Menon, sometimes the situation in the field changes in ways that even our best analysts may not foresee. In that limited timeframe, I need you to give me any kind of clearance when I ask." Menon looked at him over the rims of her glasses and pursed her lips. "Fine. I'll do whatever I can, to the best of my ability."

There was a knock at the door and a short man entered the room. "Ah, yes," murmured Radhika Menon as she stood up to shake his hand. "Pathak, meet Director Sengupta. He leads the Atomic Minerals Directorate for Exploration and Research. It's called 'AMD' for short. The AMD does the surveying, prospecting, and development of resources of uranium, thorium, lithium, beryllium, and other rare earth elements required to support our nuclear power program." Pathak clasped his hand briefly around Sengupta's pudgy fingers. Menon addressed Pathak, "We're giving extra security to Director Sengupta from now on. He will reach out to you as you proceed with your investigation. I've also given him your direct lines of contact for any emergencies. I believe there are some workers from his institute who would need to be investigated." Pathak nodded.

Menon turned to Director Sengupta and added, "I need to brief you and the Director of the Department of Atomic Energy about our security plans. The security of scientists during any kind of travel is a sensitive matter and hence it requires more attention. Normally, the security of nuclear facilities in our country is given a high priority by the specialized wing of the Central Industrial Security Forces (CISF). They also coordinate with the local administration and the police. But considering the current circumstances, we're going to have to put more plain-clothes officers in those areas." Director Sengupta sighed as she handed him a small file. As he flipped through the pages, Radhika Menon pulled Pathak aside.

She spoke in a low voice, "I'm assigning some of my men under you. If you feel compromised at any point of time during your investigations, call me right away." She gave him a short nod. "Good luck, Pathak. Keep me updated."

* * *

Alisha Nair was resting in her favourite light blue chair at home. Her delicate frame was relaxed but her mind restless. One dainty hand rested on the armrest, while the other fiddled with a small crystal paperweight. Her dark eyes noted the time on her wristwatch and her lips curled in faint annoyance.

She had just wrapped up her afternoon work meetings, but the prospect of attending yet another party in the evening irritated her. *Be careful to keep up appearances*, she reminded herself again. A party was where celebrities gathered and gossiped. For her, parties were merely comfortable places where she could observe people and gather information from the elite.

For the paparazzi, the headlines were all about who wore what. Alisha sighed. *Planning missions was easier than attending parties.* Her mind wandered, drifting away from the glittery sham and settled on the silent shadowy world that she loved as well as resented. She closed her eyes.

A vivid memory flashed in her mind. *A mole in the IB was pointing a gun at her from merely a few feet, not so long ago.* Alisha went cold as she reminisced Pramod Sharma's sneering words, *"Your father never trusted anyone, and yet he got killed."* Alisha opened her eyes, glistening with unshed tears. A cold rage began to steadily build inside her chest. *I will find my parents' killers,* she vowed silently.

She strode over to a drawer and pulled out an ancient Mickey Mouse soft toy. Her eyes lingered on the tell-tale mark of an ancient bloodstain, lightened with age, across Mickey's front. It was a reminder of her cruel past – How she had survived a horrific bomb explosion that had killed her parents.

Alisha had quite a few kills under her name, but to her, they were mere jobs. *What was the point of being a security officer when my parents' killers still walked free?* Alisha clenched her jaw. *All these years as an undercover agent... And yet, my real work of justice for myself begins now.*

* * *

Raghav Nair's hesitant hand faltered several times as he reached for the phone. *Should I really contact this man?* he wondered. He had mulled it over for several days. He finally made up his mind, *this is only in Alisha's best interests.* He took a deep breath and dialled a number, but it went unanswered. Raghav placed the phone back, feeling slightly relieved.

Barely a few moments later, the phone rang, and Raghav answered. "Hello, my boy," said a voice over the phone. The voice belonged to a certain silver-haired gentleman. "It has been a while since we talked." Raghav began to reply, but the voice cut him off, "If this is about your wife, then let us meet and talk in person." Before Raghav could respond, the line went dead.

He leaned back in his chair, his mind tangled in thoughts of what was right and what was wrong.

***

At Vishakhapatnam's naval docks, a small team worked discreetly for INS Arihant, a nuclear-powered submarine. Himesh Mathur was a technician on INS Arihant, and today something bothered him. He found himself chewing on a piece of pencil after a long time.

Mathur wiped the sweat off his brow and looked up at his colleague, Ajay Shah. "Soumik not in today too?" he asked, his tone uneasy. Shah shook his head. "Haven't seen him in a while now. Maybe the bad weather got to him." Mathur glanced up at the chunk of sky visible through the window from their naval office at the docks. An incoming cyclone had turned Visakhapatnam's peaceful skies into a stormy grey gloom for several days now.

"Should we check up on him?" asked Mathur in a worried tone. Shah looked at him sharply. "Why do you think so?" he asked. Mathur replied quietly, "Our work here at INS Arihant is classified, Ajay. We need to verify people's leaves. Being a nuclear-powered submarine, our secrets can leak out unexpectedly. We can't take any risks, especially in our team. We don't want *anything* to jeopardise INS Arihant." Shah was silent for a moment, he nodded in understanding, "Let's visit Soumik today."

But their visit never happened. Instead, Himesh Mathur and Ajay Shah were found dead on the railway tracks. Their colleague, Soumik Chandra had gone missing.

***

Soumik Chandra opened his bleary eyes and wondered hazily, *where am I?* He could hardly recollect anything from the past couple of days. His brows furrowed as he strained his memory. A pretty girl's face swam into his mind. *But what was her name? Where was she?* He couldn't remember.

As he closed his eyes, he suddenly remembered how she'd flirted with him when they'd met at a café. Even his superior, Jasveer Gujral had teased him the next day about how cheerful he looked at work. Soumik had admitted to Gujral, somewhat bashfully, that even he was just as surprised. Girls never looked his way, especially at a guy like him. Later, they'd gone to his place where she'd coyly spent the night with him. It was an experience that Soumik thought he'd never forget. She had touched him in ways that Soumik had only dreamt of.

Now, as he lay flat on his back with no memory of how he got there, Soumik wondered, *what happened to me?* His fingers brushed against a brown envelope lying on his chest. He opened it and stared at the photos. Alarm bells screamed in his head. He gasped as a phone rang right next to him, breaking the heavy silence.

Hands trembling, Soumik slowly picked it up and whispered, "Hello?" A chilling voice on the other end spoke, *"If you value your life Mr. Chandra, you will do exactly as I say..."*

CHAPTER 4

Ravi Pathak sat in his office sipping *chai* and reading the morning newspapers. A prominent international article screamed out:

'Israel strikes again at Iran's nuclear reactor'

Pathak raised his bushy eyebrows and shook his head slowly. He carefully read through the article before tossing the paper aside. The method of strike this time from Israel intrigued him. Iran's nuclear plant was underground and had been extremely well-fortified. *However, knowing the Mossad's methods...* he chuckled. His hands stretched out and wiped the top of his desk almost absently. *No need for anything else today.* He was expecting investigation reports from the R&AW today. His thoughts wandered to Radhika Menon and his expression darkened. *If only she had listened to him in Kashmir, countless lives and efforts could've been saved...* There was always a difference between the desk and the field. You couldn't know the challenges the other person faced unless you were in their shoes.

At times like these, he really missed Alisha's father, *Prakash Kamat.* Together, he and Pathak were a perfect undercover team in their younger days, almost as if reading each other's minds flawlessly. Bureaucracy had never been an issue between them. They considered themselves above the bureaucratic tussles between the two government security agencies because they completely trusted each other. Pathak sighed. *Today is one of those days when I hate the job I love.* "Some people..." he swore under his breath, finishing his *chai.*

By late morning, R&AW's reports had landed on Pathak's desk. He took a deep breath and opened the case files. The details were neatly provided, and a few hand-written notes had also been made. This was unmistakably Radhika Menon's work. Pathak's bushy eyebrows furrowed as he turned the pages slowly. He felt a sudden instinctive discomfort. *These kills were… clean. In fact, too clean.*

Pathak's desk phone rang shrilly, interrupting his thoughts. "Yes?" Pathak answered. The voice replied, "Director Sengupta of Atomic Minerals here, Pathak. We met at Radhika Menon's meeting. I'm sending you all reports that AMD has on these cases, as Radhika instructed me to." Pathak said firmly, "Yes, thank you, Director. Please ensure that you send the reports directly to me and nobody else." The director sighed, "Yes, Pathak. Solve this for me fast, will you? All this is now causing a daily chaos in my entire staff. People are noticing, and some of them are even considering resignations." He hung up.

After several hours, Pathak leant back in his chair, exhausted yet strangely alert. His hazel brown eyes blazed as he stared unseeingly at the walls, going over every single detail of R&AW's reports. This was a heap of evidence, and yet it didn't satisfy him. Years of work at the IB had kicked in a sense of urgency when he knew things were going to turn critical. His eyes passed over the names again, drawing connections, tracing patterns.

Pathak knew instinctively he needed a well-trained team for this. He needed his people to listen to whispers right from the elite circles to the shanties. *This was going to be a battle. But then,* thought Pathak rising from his chair, and striding out of his office. *When isn't it?*

* * *

Professor Saarthi finished his explanation and turned around. He beamed at the group of international exchange students listening to him in rapt attention. He asked, "So, any questions?" Several hands shot up in the air. The students in this group had arrived from various locations across South Asia, Middle East, Europe, and South America. They were visiting the Bhabha Atomic Research Centre (BARC) campus and a few other atomic plants across the country to learn the workings of different types of nuclear power plants in their advanced studies in nuclear research.

One of the students, Anya, pushed her light hair out of her eyes and peered around with interest. *The BARC was such an awesome campus*, she thought, and her eyes lit up at the thought of visiting the experimentation labs. She always loved visiting any nuclear facility. Many students from the group were staying at the campus of a university nearby. Some had already arrived here weeks before. Anya was eagerly looking forward to making new international friends.

As she walked around, soaking in Prof. Saarthi's words, she suddenly felt as though someone was watching her. She whipped around to see a handsome, cherub-faced boy staring at her. She blushed and walked towards him, working up the nerve to talk to him. Anya thought to herself, *well, he's cute. I think I have an instant crush.* She took a deep breath. "Hi, I'm Anya," she said pleasantly, extending her hand towards him. He smiled and grasped her hand lightly. He gave her hand a light kiss but did not reply. Anya noticed how his dark eyes watched her face in a way she didn't quite understand. "Well," she said jovially, swinging their hands and trying not to make things awkward. "Have you been here for long?"

"Ages," he responded quietly. *He seems to have a slightly Middle Eastern accent. Or am I wrong?* She wondered. His smile grew wider. "Can we be friends?" she asked. "Why not?" he replied, smiling widely.

"What is your name?" asked Anya. He answered in the same quiet tone, "Behzad Hashemi."

But as Anya glanced up at the Behzad's dark eyes, she suddenly felt unsure and afraid. *Or am I just overreacting?* She gave him a quick nod and walked away, feeling unnerved.

✳ ✳ ✳

Within a week, Pathak had assembled his team. His IB team members now clamoured around in his office, ready for briefing. *But the team isn't complete yet*, mused Pathak, scanning the room. A smiling Jay Bhadra sat directly in front of him. *Always enthusiastic*, noted Pathak with faint amusement. The core team members who had assisted him on his previous mission were already ready for his orders. Ankit elbowed Kapil out of his way to take the other chair, while Gopal remained standing.

"Boys," began Pathak gravely. "From the news, you've heard about the recent deaths of the nuclear scientists. Our team is going to investigate this case." His team exchanged uncertain glances. "Sir?" Jay ventured hesitantly, "But we don't usually-" Pathak interrupted him with a curt wave of his hand. "We've received specific higher orders. I know, this is a bit different for all of you than your usual work. But you are my best guys and I need everyone to work on this, considering this is of a very sensitive nature." Jay nodded.

Pathak continued, "We're looking for a very skilled assassin here. I will be assigning two of you to probe one case each. Talk to as many people as possible from the workplaces of all victims. Study the photos of the crime scene well and put your analysis in individual reports for me. Do not trust the police investigations.

In quite a few cases, the police were reluctant. The families of the victims had to fight to even get an FIR registered." His team looked at him in silence as he handed out the investigation files to them.

Ankit spoke, "Sir, we're going to need more people for this." Pathak chuckled, "Oh, we already have more people, Ankit. You just don't know them yet." *Speaking of more people, I need to see Alisha at once*, thought Pathak with a sense of urgency.

As Pathak stood up, Kapil asked him curiously, "Sir, which case are you going to investigate?" Pathak answered, "The one that intrigues me the most - Jayesh Rao."

* * *

Alisha Nair was already waiting for Ravi Pathak. Without a preamble, he slammed a dark briefcase on the wooden table. She watched him in silence, as he arranged Radhika Menon's files in a neat order and then turned to scribble notes on a whiteboard. She waited for Pathak to finish. After he was done, he turned to Alisha and said, "Ten scientists have been killed so far. One scientist is currently missing, and we don't know if he's alive. All of them have crossed each other at different points across various nuclear and space projects. The one thing common between all these victims is the Department of Atomic Energy. Now, did you finish reading the case files?" Alisha nodded, rubbing her eyes. She answered, "I have the same analysis as yours. Let's take this case by case from the beginning.

We have two young scientists who died in a fire when they were not even working with anything inflammable. They were working on retrieving cells that were damaged by radiation. There had been an incident of fire before in the same lab. Why wasn't it reported when the nuclear reactors were only one kilometre away? So, our timeline actually starts from *that unreported incident of fire*, not the deaths. Next, we take Lalith Gopalan and

Naveen Mulay. Both had once worked with the boys. The autopsy shows that Gopalan had taken blows on his internal organs and had external injuries as well. That means, he was tortured for information before he was killed.

Take Dr. Uma Rangarajan – one of the most cheerful people as reported by her colleagues. They'd gotten the approval for a new project on missiles and her two co-workers were also found dead. No other fingerprints were found on the bottle of sleeping pills beside her. Maybe that bottle was wiped clean. We also didn't find any traces of cleaning agents. So, it would make us believe that this case was simply a suicide. Now, about Jayesh Rao." She paused, deep in thought. "Yes?" asked Pathak eagerly. "There's something different about this one," Alisha said slowly, frowning.

Pathak nodded, "Jayesh Rao was found dead in his living room. At first, they thought it was a heart attack. However, someone from the government was already watching him. The forensics department have fortunately still held his body until all suspicions are ruled out. In this case, the killer had a relatively smaller window to kill and run away. Sometimes, forensics doesn't know what they're looking for. We need to *point* them to it. I will be investigating Jayesh Rao's case myself."

Alisha added, "Uncle Ravi, note that Himesh Mathur and Ajay Shah worked on INS Arihant. Mathur and Shah were poisoned and *then* left on the railway tracks. Fortunately, they were pulled away by the local people just in time from an oncoming train, but their killer did not *intend* for that to happen. So, their case, too would've probably looked like a suicide at first. And Soumik Chandra is still missing. Do we have *any* information about him?" Pathak replied, "I'm already in touch with all their superiors, Alisha. The naval office is coordinating with us on this investigation. Our teams are on the lookout for Soumik Chandra. I'm praying that we don't find his body on some god-forsaken railway tracks, too.

I'm going to talk to Jayesh Rao's family in Mumbai. I'll see you tomorrow, okay? I need you to analyse some very specific and important details after my initial investigation." Alisha nodded firmly. "I'm here for whatever you need me for. Just give me my orders." Pathak gave her a swift peck on the cheek and hurried off.

Alisha sighed deeply and stared at the photos of the youngest victims, Arjun Vasu and Pratik Bajaj, who were burnt alive in the BARC lab. Pratik came from an affluent business family, but Arjun was the sole breadwinner for his. She closed her eyes for a moment and then pulled out a cheque book from her bag. She addressed two cheques containing a very handsome amount to the families of both boys. She sealed them in envelopes and wrote Raghav's name and contact number on a separate note for any future help for Arjun's family. *Maybe Raghav can offer a job to one of Arjun Vasu's family members*, she mused. Alisha's chest tightened with sorrow.

I have learnt so much from my past. Solving her parents' murder could wait. These young boys and the other victims came first.

* * *

The Chinese MSS operative, Zheng Qui glanced at the scooters tooting their horns around her. *Kolkata*, she mused stepping into the dilapidated building, *isn't as bad as I'd thought.* She walked quietly, ensuring that nobody saw her on her way up. On the top floor, she opened the door to a spacious flat. The walls were freshly whitewashed and the windows were tinted. The space was already set up as a command centre from where she would run her operations.

Zheng Qui settled into a chair. The *right* people for this job would be arriving very soon. She'd already created a shell company named, 'Silverpoint Infra Technology Solutions'. A few other offshore accounts were ready with international funds.

She wondered when her first hurdle from the Indian government would spring up and Zheng was gearing up to meet it.

* * *

Ravi Pathak stood at the doorway of Jayesh Rao's house. His gloved hands rested on his navy-blue bag buckled at his side, checking his kit in its usual place. Pathak bent down and examined the threshold carefully. A few somber neighbours milled about. He stepped over the threshold into the living room and sat on a chair, looking around keenly. It was a neat and comfortable place with plenty of sunlight.

He stood up as Mrs. Rao entered the room. Although Pathak had spent hours examining the photos and reports, he had instinctively felt something amiss. *Something was not adding up here.* Rao was found dead on the sofa, almost as if he'd fallen asleep. If this was not a natural death, he might've spoken to his killer- and perhaps even invited them inside.

Pathak murmured empathetically, "I'm sorry for your loss, Mrs. Rao. I also deeply regret the number of times you've had to narrate this incident." Although Mrs. Rao looked pale and shaken, she composed herself. Pathak leant towards her and said gently, "I know you've said that you didn't know if Jayesh was going to meet anyone that morning. But I request you to close your eyes and remember what details were missing or moved from Jayesh's room after you found him." Mrs. Rao frowned at him and shook her head at him slowly. Pathak had expected this. She spoke slowly, "Jayesh's people from work asked me this too. I've been searching but haven't found out anything." Pathak then asked,

"Do you mind if I looked around your house for a while?" She gestured her hand towards the other rooms.

Pathak suddenly recalled the words of his old mentor, Professor Kavita Mishra. She had taught him well when he was in the IB training school.

Remember, Ravi. The absence of evidence does not imply the evidence of its absence.

It meant that any unseen or missing evidence did not mean that it was altogether absent. He just had to search for it.

Pathak took his time examining everything - room to room. *It was a death that took place on a sleepy Sunday morning... Surely, Rao invited his killer inside to have breakfast?* He strolled back to Mrs. Rao and sat in a chair facing her. Pathak spoke, "After Jayesh was pronounced dead, what did you do?" Mrs. Rao hesitated, "I... I called my brother and he rushed over here. He handled everything after that." Pathak nodded and continued, "I meant, how much do you remember about your kitchen activities on that morning?" Mrs. Rao stared at him. "I made *Pohe* for Jayesh before I stepped out that morning. After I came back and saw him..." she trailed off as she shivered at the memory.

She continued again tearfully, "That bowl of *Pohe* along with a teacup were still there in front of him." Pathak asked softly, "Do you remember if there was a second bowl or another teacup alongside his?" Mrs. Rao scrunched her face as she tried to recall. Pathak urged her gently, "I know it is difficult. But try and remember, it is very important that you do." Mrs. Rao closed her eyes. After a few moments of silence she spoke, "There was no other bowl or teacup." Pathak fell back into his chair, disappointed. *Was this a natural death, after all?* Silence fell upon the room once more.

Mrs. Rao's eyes flew open, and she sat up with her brow furrowed. "Why did you ask this question? The other police officers didn't ask me this." Pathak sighed, "There is… a *certain* angle in this death I'm not satisfied with, Mrs. Rao." Her eyes widened as she suddenly seemed to recall something.

She said, "Now that you specifically mentioned it… I had laid out *two* bowls before I left. One bowl was for Jayesh and the other one was intended for me. But when I came back, I noticed something strange that I completely ignored at that time, considering everything that happened. You see, my bowl was washed clean and kept on the shelf." Pathak sat up straight and watched her keenly. "And you didn't-" Mrs. Rao interrupted him, her voice trembling, "But Jayesh *never* washed the dishes. And I would always scold him for that. He never listened." Pathak let out a quiet sigh of satisfaction as he stared at the floor. He understood everything that had happened. *So, there was definitely a killer out there. They had just made the mistake of washing the bowl.* Mrs. Rao's eyes brimmed with tears, now realising the meaning of Pathak's questions.

Ravi Pathak sat silently for a moment, reflecting on the strange interplay of human habits. He wondered what he appreciated more at the moment – a husband's bad habit or a wife's corrective scolding.

✳ ✳ ✳

Pathak was quiet on his way back to Pune. After he reached his office, he was completely lost in thought as he stared at his white murder board. He picked up a marker and scribbled a few more notes and arrows around Jayesh Rao's name. Jay Bhadra poked his head through the door and asked, "Sir, may I come in?" Pathak nodded at him, still lost in thought. Jay came inside and sat in a chair across from him. "Sir, our investigations are baffling us all. It… well, it almost seems that they all point to multiple killers with different styles of assassination."

Pathak's glazed eyes suddenly focused on him. "Multiple killers?" repeated Pathak, frowning. Jay nodded leaning forward and said, "It would be a rather short time window to be in multiple places at once and carry out different assassinations. This is my guess, considering the evidence and timelines."

Pathak stared at his murder board again and spoke quietly, "Perhaps, Jay. Or maybe, they want us to *think* that there are multiple killers. Let's wait for all the others to send their reports back to me." Jay nodded once again recognising the dismissal and hurried out of Pathak's office. *Different assassination styles…* wondered Pathak, leaning back in his chair.

The shrill ring of the phone broke Pathak's reverie. The voice on the other line spoke, "Jaguar." Pathak sighed, "Yes, Menon." "How is the investigation going on?" she asked. Pathak chose his words carefully, "We're searching for leads, but all investigations are… misleading. Jay suspects multiple killers with different assassination styles." Radhika Menon merely replied, "I see." Pathak continued, "We haven't made any arrests as yet." Menon asked, "And what is *your* opinion?" Pathak replied evenly, "I don't know at this point. It is too early to guess." There was a brief silence when Menon spoke again, "But you have your suspicions." *It wasn't a question.* Pathak lips curved into a faint smile, "I might, but I need to test them out first before I say something."

He could almost hear Radhika Menon bristling at him. "Well, Pathak. And when are you bringing Alisha Nair into your game?" Pathak's eyes darkened and his smile faded. "What?" he snapped.

Menon chuckled lightly, "Your team is already investigating the murders. But you're on to something else with Alisha, aren't you?" It was Pathak's turn to fall silent. Menon pressed on, "She's your best, isn't she? I want Alisha here at the headquarters the day after tomorrow. *Alone.* She will train with me for at least two weeks.

Someone will receive her at the airport." She disconnected the call, leaving Pathak staring into the distance, with an uneasy feeling.

* * *

Alisha Nair was at home, poring over the reports when Pathak barged into her room. "I don't like it," he spat. "I don't like it one bit."

Alisha sprang up from her chair, looking concerned. "What happened, Uncle Ravi?" she asked. Pathak glared at her, "Radhika Menon wants you at the R&AW headquarters day after tomorrow." Alisha held up her hands. "Wait, hold on for a second, Uncle Ravi. *Who* is this, Radhika Menon?"

Pathak sighed and slumped into a chair. "Radhika Menon is from the R&AW. I worked with her in Kashmir against ISI operatives in very sensitive areas in the Kashmir valley. She nearly compromised me. This was many years ago when I was much younger." Alisha's eyes widened and she opened her mouth to speak, but Pathak paid her no heed and continued, "From the R&AW, Radhika Menon is leading the investigation on the murders of our nuclear scientists. She was the one who handed us these cases in the first place. She wanted me to lead from the Intelligence Bureau." Alisha nodded in understanding; brows still furrowed. "And Menon wants me at the R&AW. Why?" Pathak shrugged and retorted, "She said that she wants to train you."

Alisha's eyes gleamed. "Then she'll see me the day after tomorrow." Pathak raised an eyebrow at her. "How much do you know about the Indian nuclear program, Alisha?" he asked her, frowning slightly. Alisha looked at him in surprise. "What do you mean?" she asked.

Pathak asked her in a clipped tone, "Who killed our scientists and displaced our nuclear programs at the very beginning?"

Alisha thought for a moment and answered, "Well, let's start with Dr. Homi Bhabha's murder in 1966. The CIA killed him. Dr. Bhabha died 18 days after announcing that India could build an atomic bomb in 3 months. But then, he was killed just 13 days after Lal Bahadur Shastri's murder, so both deaths are connected along the lines of nuclear power. And I'm guessing that Dr. Vikram Sarabhai did not die of natural causes, either."

"Yes, but did you consider the other agencies involved in the killings after that? And I mean the killings that have happened since 2005?" Pathak asked with scrutinizing eyes.

Alisha shook her head. "I actually don't know much about the murders of our nuclear scientists, *Kaka*," she admitted. "There aren't many accessible case files either. All I know is that the CIA admitted to planting a bomb on Dr. Homi Bhabha's plane. And in recent times, a lot of foreign agencies are massively involved in the killings. Everybody stands to gain by bringing India's nuclear projects down."

Pathak rubbed his palms over his tired eyes and spoke, "Do you know, the CIA had once installed a nuclear-powered sensing device in our Himalayas?" Alisha gawked at him in disbelief. Pathak continued, "Yes, it happened in around 1967, codenamed as operation HAT. Somewhere in the Himalayas, near the peak of the Nanda Devi, the CIA had installed a small nuclear-powered device to spy on China supposedly without the prime minister's permission. It was a nuclear power pack filled with plutonium 238, buried in the snow and rocks. The plutonium power pack was to remain in the Himalayas until it deteriorated, becoming a radioactive menace that could have leaked into the snow and subsequently into the Ganga.

From what I've heard, the CIA had even specifically demanded our agencies to keep this a secret from Indira Gandhi. Due to storms and avalanches, the device even got lost somewhere in the Himalayas." Alisha stared at him wide eyed and indignant. Pathak shrugged and continued, "Well, our Atomic Energy Commission tested the Ganga's waters. Thankfully, there was zero contamination." Alisha snapped, "And who carried out the tests? Were they cross-checked if the CIA bribed them to say so?" Pathak shook his head ruefully and said, "All those investigating officers are now either dead or very old, and they don't disclose anything about those cases. It was all hushed up very well, Alisha. Just like the Kerala mining case." Alisha raised her eyebrows questioningly and gave him a wary look.

Pathak continued, "The sanctions that America had imposed on us included a ban on mining the thorium-enriched areas particularly in Kerala. We were not allowed to mine our *own* resources. And later, we got to know that America was carrying out discreet mining operations on those same areas through the sand mafia." Alisha looked disgusted and was silent for a long time.

Pathak spoke again, "There are also rumours that when British controlled India, there were reports of rare earth minerals in Gilgit-Baltistan. Apparently, there was a secret meeting conducted between Mountbatten and other high-ranking British officers in Britain about this. This was yet another reason why there was more focus on the British breaking apart Kashmir. They thought it would be an advantage to them sometime down the future. Then again, that meeting was never made public.

There's also a lot of mystery surrounding our secret projects on missiles. Do you remember project Devil that led to the Prithvi missile in the 1980s?" Alisha shook her head.

Pathak's brown eyes became distant as he seemed to recollect an old memory while he continued, "My friend's father, T. Venkataramaiah was a chief scientist in the Geological Survey of India. His work was in the Krishna Godavari basin which is upwards of rupees 32 million of government property. T. Venkataramaiah was an officer from the civil services batch of 1971. Some years ago, a local corporator and 15 gang members broke into my friend's house and killed his parents. There was no police enquiry or official statement issued on the death of his parents. His father had surprisingly declared project Devil as a failure. Although, project Devil is still a very powerful project in missiles technology, and nobody seems to know its formula other than some very high-ranking military officers. My friend complained to the higher authorities in the central government, but the police commissioner from his jurisdiction used his influence on the higher authorities to close the case.

There was a ruling chief minister related to the Krishna Godavari basin who was killed in a helicopter crash. A Russian newspaper, in fact, had reported that the business mafia killed the chief minister in Kakinada, Andhra Pradesh. One never knows the truth, you know."

Alisha finally spoke, "Really, *Kaka*… The more I learn, the more I realize how much I don't know. Sometimes, I even feel like I just don't want to know all this." Pathak gave a sad chuckle. Alisha's head fell back in comtemplation.

Pathak spoke with a softened expression, "Look, here. Before you go to the R&AW headquarters Alisha, I need to brief you about many things. The R&AW functions very differently from the Intelligence Bureau. It even evolves everyday… In fact, much more than we do at the Intelligence Bureau." Pathak gave a dry chuckle. "Consider this a small training *before* your training."

Alisha shook her head and gave him a weary smile. *Life could be unexpectedly amusing, sometimes.*

* * *

Raghav Nair was sipping a cup of coffee when he felt Alisha's arms wrap around him. He set down the mug of steaming coffee and pulled her right into his lap. He held her there, their noses gently grazing against each other.

Alisha gave him a long kiss and drew back. Raghav gazed at her melancholy expression and asked, "What's the matter?" She replied, "I'm being called to Delhi. I'll be away for two weeks." Raghav took a deliberate sip of his coffee and murmured, "But you're coming back, right?" She ran her fingers through his dark hair and chuckled softly, "I always come back. And your hair's getting longer. Make sure you get a haircut while I'm away."

He gazed at her for a long time and said nothing. He finally gave a small sigh, hugged her tightly, and buried his nose into her neck, breathing against her skin, "Fine, I will." Alisha gave a shiver of pleasure as he lightly stroked the nape of her neck. She leaned into his touch, her lips curving into a small smile.

Raghav cupped her face and whispered, "I'll miss you, darling. Come back soon. And since I'm free for the next hour..." Smirking, he jerked his head towards the bedroom. She grinned at him. He pushed the coffee aside and carried her upstairs into their bedroom.

✳ ✳ ✳

The nuclear research exchange student, Anya smiled at the young, cherubic face of Behzad who was from the Middle East. Ever since their visit to the BARC, she had made friends with him now and even had a secret crush on him. *He's so cute*, thought Anya coyly. They were at his place, and they'd just finished eating snacks.

They'd been talking and meeting for several weeks now and Anya felt comfortable taking their relationship to the next level. They were at the same campus together. The international exchange program had brought her many friends, but she felt that he was the most special among them all. Though she felt close to Behzad, she felt as if she didn't know him at all. He never talked about his family back home like everyone else did.

Anya noticed his black eyes watching her as she took off her shirt and put her arms around his neck. She pulled him into a deep kiss, and he responded by seizing her into his arms. He carried her to his old bed, and threw her down, not bothering to be gentle. *If she only knew who I am, or even what I am...* he thought as he unzipped his jeans. *If she did, she would run away from this place, screaming in terror.* That very thought of her being terrified of him made him erect. He had no patience to caress her. *She knew what she's come here for, and I'm going to give it to her good.*

Her eyes flew open at first in excitement and then closed as Behzad locked her hands above her head. He bit into her neck and his fingers groped at her, ravenously squeezing every inch of her. Without warning, he plunged into her. She gasped and her eyes flew open. As he thrust harder and harder, he started shaking. Anya gazed into his eyes, transfixed. Despite the heat between them, she felt a chill run down her spine. She was suddenly very afraid, and she couldn't understand why.

Behzad hadn't noticed that her flailing limbs and arching back had suddenly gone rigid. As he came close to climaxing, Anya felt as though a demon was looking right back at her through those charcoal-black eyes that she had once felt were cute. Panting, he pulled out of her and rolled away. She lay there, staring at the ceiling, realisation dawning slowly on her. *Who is this boy? I feel as though I don't know him at all.*

Her feminine instincts suddenly seemed to warn her, *get out of here, now.*

Anya quickly sat up and got dressed in complete silence. She realised how his attitude had now turned cold.

Behzad could see the conflict and confusion raging in Anya's eyes. Her vulnerability ignited something primal within him. Watching her getting dressed, all scared, made him feel triumphant.

I've killed so many before, laid their bodies on railway tracks, arranged so many deaths to look like suicides... I feel no emotions when I kill... Because I kill dispassionately. And now, killing this girl would be so easy, that she wouldn't even know when death hit her.

But something kept him from charging at her. He was not instructed to kill her. *Her jugular was so close to him... It would take hardly a few minutes.* However, Anya suddenly turned and hurried out of the door. She did not look back at him. As he watched her slim legs disappear, his black eyes still yearned with a desire to kill.

The cherub-faced assassin, Behzad Hashemi slammed the door after her and smiled. His thirst to kill had suddenly awoken again.

CHAPTER 5

Alisha Nair glanced at the nondescript white building that housed the R&AW's operational quarters. With a jolt of pain, she suddenly realised, *this was where my father must've once worked.*

She went over Uncle Ravi's words once more. *The workings of the R&AW change almost every day, Alisha. Now, I don't know what Radhika Menon exactly wants from you. Maybe she's doing this to keep an eye on me. I don't like to say this, but don't trust her unit completely. If she unexpectedly springs something on you, don't flounder and panic. Stay calm and analyse everything you see or hear at the R&AW.*

Two men walked over to her. The taller among the two enquired, "Alisha Nair?" She nodded. He replied, "I'm Mr. Trivedi. I will escort you upstairs." She followed them inside the premises, her heart pounding slightly in anticipation.

Half an hour later, Alisha was sitting across from Radhika Menon. Both women watched each other shrewdly for several moments before Menon spoke, "I assume Pathak has already briefed you about everything?" Alisha answered, "Yes." Menon continued, "You will be briefed again by the agency during your training. Excellent work on your last mission… The way you handled everything was impressive." Alisha did not reply.

Menon leant forward. "Both, you, and Ravi must be wondering why I brought you in. I know you would be at the centre of Ravi's plans, Alisha. And I want you to be prepared whenever that time comes. These murders…" she shook her head in distaste and continued, "There are unforeseen external dangers in these cases. We're battling people and agencies across borders operating in the shadows, as well as shell companies that exist everywhere, committed to conducting expert financial frauds. I do predictive analysis for all my cases. My analysis is that our enemy will make a move soon. From my understanding of you, your experience, your psychology, and your relationship with Ravi, I think you're the right person for these cases. And I'm going to put you in the right place at the right time."

Alisha studied Menon intently and asked, "And what exactly do you expect from me?"

Radhika Menon laughed. This time, it was a much warmer laugh. "I'm going to train you very well here at R&AW. Make no mistake, it will be rigorous. It will be different from what you've trained for so far. And I'm not training you to handle just this mission. I'm training you for your future, as well. I think you're already an excellent asset. You just need some training from R&AW's perspective. I want to train you particularly on geostrategic analysis." She paused and eyed her once more before she spoke, "I don't know what Ravi has warned you about me, Alisha. But I think you and I are going to enjoy working together much more than me and him."

Alisha merely smiled; her thoughts unreadable.

＊＊＊

A week and a half into her R&AW training, Alisha found her head drooping with exhaustion as she studied her investigation report. A quick glance at her watch revealed it was 2 a.m., but the night wasn't over yet.

She had shadowed a small group of people in the late afternoon and was composing an analysis report on them.

Alisha enjoyed training with the R&AW even though it was intense. Radhika Menon was right – it was different from what she'd trained for so far. This training was hard, but interesting. Alisha had been extensively trained with the Intelligence Bureau's way of doing things. With the Research and Analysis Wing, her training was much more diverse and sophisticated.

She'd already aced R&AW's physical and tactical training. Growing up with Ravi Pathak, her psychological training had also been rigorous. But now, Alisha was being groomed to focus on a set of highly specific sectors, all related to nuclear energy. She was also taught a wide range of subjects, from India's current foreign and geostrategic policies to the latest techniques in espionage.

The chair next to her creaked as a tall man sank into it with a tired sigh. "Not sleepy yet, Trivedi?" Alisha asked cheerfully. Radhika Menon had assigned Trivedi to Alisha's team. "We poor men can sleep only after the madam in command is satisfied." Alisha raised a curious brow at him. Trivedi bent down to Alisha's ear level as he picked up her pen. He seemed to examine it with great interest. As Alisha looked up at him curiously, he murmured very softly, "Your father worked here once upon a time. We'll talk about this later at the right time."

Alisha froze. As Trivedi set her pen down, he gave her a slight smile and walked away. All her sleep seemed to fly right out of the window. Her mind raced as she stared blankly at the white walls that cast long, looming dark shadows. *Her father used to work here. Prakash Kamat.* It took her a long time to recollect her thoughts.

She finished writing her report and tossed her pen aside. She wished she could speak to someone about her father. As she rubbed her eyes, she suddenly missed Raghav. She wondered what her husband was doing right now.

* * *

Raghav Nair tilted his head as he stared at the silver-haired gentleman, codenamed 'Dhruv'. The man smoothened the cuffs of his crisp white shirt. His eyes met Raghav's, and he gave him a patient smile that seemed to reflect the wisdom gathered in his greying years.

"So, do we have a deal then, Nair?" he asked. Raghav's brows furrowed and his jaw hardened as he gazed at the dark coffee table, pondering. Accepting such a deal would be a long commitment. And yet, if he didn't accept the deal, he would miss out on the chance of a lifetime. Raghav found himself at crossroads – he didn't know whether this was the right decision or the wrong one.

Think about Alisha. Her beautiful face floated in front of him. *She was doing so much already.*

"We have a deal," said Raghav finally, looking up. The silver-haired gentleman leant back in his rich leather armchair and gave him a wide smile.

***

The door to Pathak's office burst open as Jay Bhadra came sprinting inside. "Sir, we have an update on the missing scientist," he panted, skidding to a halt before Pathak's desk. "Soumik Chandra was spotted in Chennai's railway station. I've already alerted the IB teams there." Pathak sprang up. "How soon can they get him here?" Jay replied, "They will need a few hours, sir."

Pathak seized his desk phone and continued to shout instructions at Jay. "Alert the southern railway security Jay, and ready our team. Check all the departing trains where he was spotted. We're heading to Chennai right away. Soumik Chandra is someone who needs protection as soon as possible. He would be fearing for his life and he'll try any medium to escape from the city." Jay Bhadra nodded and rushed off.

Pathak murmured quick words into the phone to Radhika Menon. He was glad that Alisha was returning home tomorrow from her R&AW training. He would need her when they would question Soumik Chandra.

* * *

Ravi Pathak wiped the sweat off his forehead and glanced up at the gentle blue Chennai sky. They'd travelled as fast they could to Chennai, but it had still taken them several hours to reach the city. An alert had already been issued for Soumik Chandra's whereabouts, and their IB team had fanned across the city. Pathak's cellphone vibrated in his pocket, and he answered it immediately. It was Ankit.

"Sir, we received fresh intel that Soumik Chandra was just spotted in the Velachery area. It seems he's cancelled his train plans. He might be waiting for the next bus that would take him out of the city." Pathak spoke urgently, "Are you near that area?" Ankit replied, "Yes, sir." Pathak continued in an urgent tone, "Then search for him Ankit, and be very careful. He's part of a highly sensitive project and others might be after him. He will not trust you right away. I'm on my way to you now."

Thirty minutes later, when Pathak and his team reached the Velachery area, a scene of destruction met their eyes. A bomb blast had occurred just before they'd arrived. Pathak stared around in horror at the destroyed bus stand and the burning tyres of a parked bus. People shrieked and collided into each other. Pathak quickly assessed the scene. Despite the hysteria around him, Pathak forced himself to calm his mind and quickly assess the situation.

No dead bodies here, he realised. *Only a few injuries on some people. That previous bus had already departed, so this blast was either hastily arranged or poorly planned. But where was Ankit?*

"Ankit, where are you?" shouted Pathak, racing through the dark smoke. "Ankit, can you hear me?" He pulled out his phone and dialled the nearest police station. When the phone connected, he shouted instructions into it. By then, the rest of his team had arrived. Jay, Kapil, Gopal and a few others raced over, looking equally shaken. Pathak's heart thudded with growing dread and anguish. *If anything happened to Ankit…*

"Sir, here," shouted Kapil from behind a large, fallen board. Pathak sprinted over to see Ankit stirring. The blast had thrown him into a wall and had knocked him unconscious. Pathak swiftly assessed his injuries. Other than bruises and scratches, Ankit seemed fine. Pathak gave a cry of relief and threw his arms around Ankit. *The poor boy…*

He and Kapil together hoisted him up and carried him out. An ambulance screeched to a halt nearby and they carried Ankit over to the van. Two paramedics took over, put Ankit on a stretcher, and administered first aid. Pathak watched them anxiously. One of the paramedics glanced up and asked, "How many casualties are there?" Pathak replied, "None, thankfully." He pointed them to a few injured people across from him. "But they're injured and will need first aid."

He beckoned to Jay Bhadra and spoke with an urgency in a much lower voice, "Search for Soumik Chandra. This blast must've been for him. I'm praying that we don't find his body here."

CHAPTER 6

Somewhere in Kolkata, the Chinese MSS operative, Zheng Qui nodded in satisfaction as her eyes skimmed the newspaper. She eagerly turned a few more pages to see a particular article. She took a long sip of her black tea as her narrow eyes scanned the page. *There it was...*

Zheng had paid a handsome amount to a popular journalist to write an article glorifying the Naxalite movement. An exclusive interview of a Naxal leader was splashed across the entire page, highlighting their cause. The carefully crafted narrative was a perfect tool to stoke unrest. Zheng turned the pages and smiled as her fingers lingered over an advertisement that encouraged the use of Chinese products.

Zheng was a meticulous planner. Her next steps were already mapped out. She decided that the next article would be rolled out after a fortnight. Zheng had already routed money through Silverpoint Infra Tech Solutions to that Naxal leader and the Maoist political party for further activities against India. She had also sent handsome amounts to ISI's sleeper cells and their political subsidiaries. She would be needing their services very soon. Every pawn had been moved into its place.

I have planned everyone's tasks well, she thought as she allowed herself a rare moment of satisfaction. *The more unrest it causes, the better.*

***

The man called Knight received a phone call. A mysterious voice asked, "Is the next plan of action ready?" Knight replied, his tone impassive, "Yes, it is ready. Everything has been arranged. The web has been spun. My pawn is already on the move." The line disconnected abruptly.

Knight was expecting his payment after this chunk of work was over. He leant back and reflected on his grim past. *How many times did he have to beg and grovel in the dirt for favours?* Knight swore to himself, *it will never happen again. After my work is over, I will be celebrated and rewarded justly as an indispensable asset.* Knight had dreamt of making it big in life ever since he was a child. He already had plans to wind up his business and move. *How many times had he done this before? How many times had he killed people doing it?* But Knight didn't care. To him, it was his world, and every move was justified in it.

He reminisced his days in America when he'd gained admission to a reputed university. His mother had been so proud of him. Knight admired the wonderful diversity that America offered. *I could leave all my problems back at home. The days of unrest have ended for me in this new land…* Until he met a Pakistani professor in one of his classes. He had admired Professor Farooqi's intellect and teaching style. And the hardworking student had become one of the professor's favourites. They would often enjoy discussing economics for several hours.

However, when Professor Farooqi asked about his home, Knight would fall silent and change the topic. He would silently remind himself; *I can't go back there. I've made my peace with it.* But Professor Farooqi continued to coax him. They were so close, that the professor would invite him to his home for dinner. Knight enjoyed the professor's special Biryani. And every day, the professor would probe him gently but firmly, "Tell me what's in your heart, my boy… only I am your family here. I'm always there for you. And I will wait until you're ready to tell me."

One day, they were eating sandwiches sitting in the university's café. Knight was silent for a long time. He finally blurted out the truth. Knight told the professor, "Professor Farooqi, I am from Kashmir. I want nothing to do with my hometown now. It is a very touchy topic for me. My father's death broke my family, especially my mother. So, forgive me if I don't speak about it." The professor had listened carefully. His gentle nod of understanding and comforting hand on Knight's shoulders seemed to convey everything. A grateful Knight had hurried away to his next class, but the professor remained in his seat, staring after him with a hard expression in his eyes.

In the days that followed, Knight had failed to notice the subtle change in Professor Farooqi's attitude towards him. The professor's gentle facade had melted away to reveal a shrewd and controlling ISI recruiter. Slowly, Farooqi started introducing him to some Pakistani friends over dinners. They would invite Knight over to their place and everyone would invariably end up discussing the Kashmir issue until midnight. And Knight's resentment would start boiling all over again. It would all boil down to the same question over and over again. *Don't you Kashmiris want Azaadi from India? We can help you get it.*

And finally, Knight had been won over. Resentment began to simmer. *After all, this is what my father had given his life for,* he often thought. Professor Farooqi had connected him to a few other clandestine individuals who had trained Knight well. In fact, Knight could never have even dreamt that Professor Farooqi could have such high connections. He had introduced him to the very people whose existence Knight had only heard of. Knight had never even realised when Professor Farooqi had turned him into a pawn. They had overturned all the things that Knight had made peace with. And finally, Knight was ready to come back to India. They had promised him that his actions would cement Kashmir's independence from India. Mumbai would be just the beginning of one of his controlling centers. Delhi and a few others would be next. A list of cities had been readied for him. And Knight was now determined to impress them all.

Knight swore to Professor Farooqi, '*All those terrible days that my brothers suffered will be avenged. And I'll be the one to deliver justice.*'

***

A few days later, Ravi Pathak was pacing up and down in his office, tension radiating from him like a storm. His team stared at him almost mechanically, following his movements. Pathak stopped suddenly and turned towards them sharply. "What do you mean, Soumik Chandra is *gone*? There was no dead body in that blast radius, and we searched everywhere. We alerted all the IB units from the states that Soumik Chandra could've reached. How could he just disappear when so many teams were on the lookout for him?"

Gopal cleared his throat and spoke hesitantly, "Sir, the Popular Front of India group has claimed responsibility for this blast. The local IB units are already investigating this Jihadi organisation. Do you think we should share our intel with the local investigating unit?" Pathak pondered for a moment, and said slowly, "No. Let them do their own investigations. We will assist only on a need-to-know basis. We don't know anything about this blast as yet. It was definitely targeted at Soumik Chandra and us. But the lesser those local IB units know about Chandra, the better. Keep his name out of it. I don't know whom to trust in there at this point. At least we know one head of the monster now. So, we can start tracing the faces and identities behind all this."

Jay Bhadra looked glum as he shrugged and asked, "Sir maybe-" But Pathak's desk phone interrupted him. Pathak seized it and spoke tersely, "Yes, tell me you have something." It was Radhika Menon on the other line.

"What?" said Pathak blankly. He listened intently, and slowly put the phone down, staring at it with an unreadable expression.

His team was visibly tensed before Pathak turned to them and spoke in quiet tones.

"Soumik Chandra has escaped India's borders."

* * *

Radhika Menon was already speaking to Alisha on the phone when Pathak barrelled into her room. Alisha's eyes flashed with a sense of urgency, and her free hand was scribbling down quick notes with practiced precision. *Menon is going to put her out there now*, realised Pathak with dread as he stared at Alisha's determined face. He had already understood what was going to happen and wondered how it was going to be played out. *We cannot afford to lose any more time.*

When Alisha finally hung up the phone and turned to Pathak, he asked her only one terse question, "Where?"

Alisha replied unflinchingly, "Istanbul."

* * *

In Tel Aviv, Katriel Levy felt serene as she reclined in her chair. *Another day, another win.* The Mossad had accomplished their mission in Iran by thwarting their nuclear progress, yet again. But a shrill phone call shattered her tranquility. Katriel's eyes widened as she listened to the orders of the Deputy Chief of the Mossad on the other line. After she put down the phone, she swore at the top of her voice.

Fifteen minutes later, Ben Shapiro sat across her, listening to her entire report. Katriel ran a frustrated hand through her hair and stared at him, hard. "This is one of the Hamas leaders we are dealing with. Abu Tawil isn't like the others. He's calculated, elusive, and always one step ahead at all times. He seems to be up to something very sinister. We need someone over there. Are you ready?" she asked. Ben simply nodded, his face calm and resolute.

She continued, "Then, pack your bags. You're leaving for Istanbul."

CHAPTER 7

Istanbul, Turkey

Alisha Nair gazed up at the towering minarets of the Hagia Sophia, their majesty illuminated by the golden sunlight. Her eyes took in its surroundings as she strolled past the monument. *Once Constantinople, now Istanbul*, she mused. Her flight to Istanbul had been uneventful. She remembered Uncle Ravi's tensed face before she'd left. Back home, her team members were in a rush to prepare themselves for any possibility. *Now the fun begins,* she thought wryly. *So, Soumik Chandra was a traitor. The man had gotten on a trawler and escaped India's borders.* Even Alisha couldn't help but resentfully admire his daring way of escape. Unfortunately for Soumik Chandra, someone had spotted him along the way and had reported him to the IB.

Alisha glanced at her watch. She had an hour to reach the city centre to meet her team. People smiled at her as they walked past. A cold trickle on her wrist drew her attention and she glanced down. Her *Dondurma*, as the locals called it, or Turkish ice cream as the tourists called it, was melting. She wiped the back of her hand with a tissue, then smiled faintly. She liked Istanbul; it was a pretty and colourful city. *I should bring Raghav here someday.* Alisha had left a quick note for him at home. He'd had a business meeting in another city, but she'd already left before he came back. *Can't afford to lose any time,* she reminded herself grimly.

She felt something brush her legs and glanced down, startled. An orange cat had twined itself around her legs and was rubbing its head contentedly against her legs. Alisha reached down and scratched it around the ears, chuckling when it purred loudly. She dipped a finger into her ice cream and offered it to the cat. It eagerly licked the melting ice cream off her finger. *Really, this city is owned by cats, not people*, she thought amusedly.

An hour later, Alisha had reached the city centre. She walked into a coffee shop named *'Viyana Kahvesi'* and sat down at one of the tables. She carefully scanned the room for any listening devices. Satisfied, she leaned back and waited. A few minutes later, three men walked into the shop. They spotted Alisha, walked over to her, and greeted her like an old friend. *Assets are hidden everywhere*, she thought with mild amusement, though her expression remained composed. They introduced themselves as Jalal, Satya, and Paul. *Nice codenames*, she chuckled internally and ordered coffees for all of them.

Alisha then leaned forward and murmured, "I understand that you're tracking our... *shipment*?" She meant Soumik Chandra. Satya nodded and replied, "Yes. It has arrived here, and we have identified it. We're expecting that it will proceed to Hotel Divan tomorrow. We suspect that there are some other shipments arriving there as well. However, until all the shipments arrive at Hotel Divan, we are not to engage. The hotel isn't very far from here." Alisha frowned and asked in a low voice, "Why can't we just conduct an extraction?" Satya shook his head. "Unless we know who's meeting him, we'll never get to the bottom of things. We need to interrogate those people as well. We just rush in at the right time." Alisha raised an eyebrow, "So, we're using our shipment as bait?" Satya did not reply.

Alisha narrowed her eyes and nodded reluctantly. "I'll check out the hotel. We need to work on a plan for tomorrow." She took a sip of her coffee and choked. The brew was too strong for her liking.

Jalal gave her a faint smile. "We'll take you to our... *warehouse*. We can plan there."

* * *

Alisha placed her hand on the railings of the rickety wooden steps. *So, Soumik Chandra was staying at this inn*, she thought, glancing around at the stained-glass windows, puzzled. *An interesting choice.*

Alisha had disguised herself as a teenage boy. She slowly ascended the creaky stairs, balancing the tray of coffee in her other hand. As she reached the landing, she saw a man standing outside Chandra's door. As he glanced back at her, Alisha pretended to proceed to the second floor. His sharp, deep blue eyes moved away from her. She hid herself on the stairs and peered at the landing below her. The man stood motionless for a long time.

Alisha wondered if she should confront him. Just as she got up from the stairs, the man turned and hurried away. Alisha's breath hitched as she stood hidden under the dull yellow lamp that cast a shadow on the man's sharp features. Alisha watched the back of the man with narrowed eyes. The fading light from the window however caught the tell-tale sign of Ben Shapiro's light golden hair hidden under his maroon cap.

Alisha froze as the door next to Chandra's opened. A thickset bodyguard with a gun intently watched the retreating man wearing the maroon cap. Ben Shapiro did not realise that he was compromised. The bodyguard's cruel mouth curved into an eerie smile as he slowly closed the door. *Who was this gunman?* Her heart thudded uncomfortably.

After what seemed like several hours, Alisha rose noiselessly and slipped out of the inn. At a considerable distance, she sprinted away as fast as she could.

* * *

"Our cargo is on the move," murmured Jalal in Alisha's ear. Soumik Chandra had started for Hotel Divan. Disguised today as an elderly Turkish lady, Alisha wove in and out of the crowd watching Chandra. *What the hell was he up to? Who was he even meeting? Did he not know that his life was in danger?*

They'd planned to apprehend him after he finished his meeting at Hotel Divan. As they turned around the corner, Alisha was startled as she noticed a familiar face. The golden haired, blue-eyed stranger that she'd seen yesterday outside Chandra's room was now walking down the street. Alisha noticed that this time, he had hidden himself well, but she'd recognised him through his disguise. She wondered if they should have two targets today instead of one.

Chandra disappeared into the hotel. He didn't seem to be in a hurry. Her team member, Paul was already sitting in the lobby. He glanced up from his newspapers as Chandra crossed him. Alisha took a seat in front of Paul. Fifteen minutes later, Satya joined them, his face pale.

Satya murmured, "We have a problem. They're on the fourth floor, in room 405. There are *four* armed guards with Chandra. I managed to get a photo of one of the guards before he went inside the room. He's from a banned organisation. I've alerted my contacts in the Indian embassy. I think they might be able to find out where this guard lives, but it will take some time. We can search his place later."

Alisha spoke quietly, "We're going to have to wait for Chandra. We can't get him out without making a scene here-" She stopped mid-way as she spotted the golden-haired man slip discreetly up the hotel's stairwell. *Was he a part of Chandra's meeting, too?*

Alisha continued in a low voice, "Alright, guard all the exits of the hotel. I told you I spotted this man yesterday. He's back. If he's here to meet Chandra, then I'm interested in him, too."

Alisha quietly followed him to the fourth floor, careful to remain unnoticed. The stranger disappeared into room 406, next to Chandra's. *Were the rooms internally connected?* Frustration bubbled within her. Alisha wished that she could plant listening devices inside. They hadn't gained access to the CCTV cameras yet. But she was sure that the footage would be blurry. *If I could only catch a glimpse of what's happening inside,* she thought with desperation. She moved slowly up the long corridor. It had been nearly an hour since Chandra had gone inside.

At first, Alisha did not notice the smoke. But when the long, white tendrils slowly engulfed her, she realised that they were originating from room 405. *Soumik Chandra was getting killed in a fire,* she thought in panic. She decided to break down the door as the fire alarms went off around her. Suddenly, the door to room 406 flew open and the golden-haired stranger appeared in the doorway. Alisha quickly dived behind one of the housekeeping trolleys, just as the door to room 405 swung open. Three armed thickset bodyguards stood in the doorway, and for a moment they locked eyes with the golden-haired stranger. The tension broke like a snapped wire.

The stranger sprang away from the door and pulled out his gun, but the nearest guard punched him in his stomach and landed a kick squarely between his legs, bringing him to his knees. As another held him down, the third guard rammed the butt of his gun into the back of the stranger's head. Alisha watched silently as the guard dragged the unconscious stranger into room 405. As his feet disappeared into the room, the door closed behind him.

She hesitated, and then ran downstairs to the others. On the way, she barelled into Satya. She shouted over the shrill fire alarm. "That golden-haired man was dragged inside the room. They're way better armed than we are." Satya shook his head as people jostled them on their way to flee to safety. He shouted, "There's something wrong… why hasn't the fourth floor been evacuated yet?" They stared at the small crowd. Chandra was nowhere to be seen. A tumultuous, sick feeling echoed in the pit of Alisha's stomach. *It could only mean one thing…*

"Chandra has escaped the hotel," shouted Paul as he raced past them. Alisha felt utterly stupid. *It was a set-up. The fire had just been a distraction.*

Satya thrust a note in her hand and spoke urgently, "Take this. The embassy just replied with the last known location of that gunman. It might possibly be the address of their hideout. This location was already flagged on their radar. We'll search for Chandra here once and join you over there. Go, just go – We need to spread out in all possible locations right now." Alisha barely registered his words as she raced out into the street.

* * *

Alisha crouched in the room, her sharp eyes fixed on the black car approaching the building. She had reached the address that Satya had given to her and had carefully broken into the house.

Alisha took deep breaths to calm herself down. *I am in the safehouse of a group of assassins.* Watching from a window, she observed four men drag out the golden-haired stranger. *Satya's hunch about the address had paid off*, thought Alisha. The stranger seemed to be barely conscious, but he was still putting up a fight.

They will be here in five minutes. I'm already compromised, she realised.

She dove under a large bed, wiping the beads of sweat that were now rolling down her temple. The front door to the flat burst open, and there seemed to be a struggle at the door. Alisha peered from the slit under her hiding place. They threw the bruised and battered stranger into a chair and tied his hands and feet. *But Soumik Chandra was nowhere to be seen.* She wondered where her team was.

The man who seemed to be the group's commander gave an exalted cry as he finally took off his black mask and threw it aside. Alisha stared in shock. Her blood ran cold. *Wasn't this Abu Tawil? He was wanted by Interpol and several other agencies for terror attacks in Europe. Wasn't he a part of the terror organisation Hizb-Ut-Tahrir, too? And now, he stood mere feet away from her.*

All the men had guns slung across their thickset backs. Abu Tawil slapped the stranger tied in the chair with such force, that the chair rocked to one side. He dragged the chair into the other room, but Alisha could still hear them. She guessed that they would torture him for some time. The other men now put down their guns and moved about in the room. She tried to steady her jittery nerves.

Alisha studied the faces of the gunmen in silence. She knew now that getting to the golden-haired stranger was the key to Soumik Chandra. *And if he doesn't talk… then I need another source of information.* She profiled the face of one guard that had a certain element of reluctance. She fingered the syringe hidden in her pocket, glad that she was carrying her set of delicate weapons. Alisha prayed that this entire situation wouldn't turn into a diplomatic disaster. *Be calm, don't panic.*

The stranger suddenly gave a blood-curdling scream from the inner room. *They were beginning to have their fun with him now.* Alisha closed her eyes.

$$* * *$$

Ben Shapiro felt as if all hope seemed lost.

Blood poured down Ben's face as he sat restrained and desolate. His trained mind pushed him to think through the haze of searing pain from where they'd tortured him.

Ben Shapiro looked tiredly into the eyes of his killer. He knew that Abu Tawil could not be negotiated with. He knew his exact type. This man was a rabid dog. He wondered if the dog would think of handing him over to his master. Ben broke into a sweat. *It would be one of the most disastrous hostile negotiations of the year. One Mossad agent for the release of countless Jihadis.* Or worse, arm-twisting Israel into a geopolitical deal.

But, Ben wondered if it was prudent to die instead. *How had they known about his identity?* There was no way he could get out of this situation yet. His kidnappers weren't stupid, they had carefully stripped all the tracking pieces off him. A Sayeret Matkal unit would be searching for him right now, but it would be too late by the time they arrived. Ben knew he couldn't stall the rabid dog towering over him. These men were very well armed, and Ben knew that his entire Sayeret Matkal team would be compromised in case of a shootout. He preferred to die alone instead of putting his entire team in danger. *How had his end come to this?*

The dark red stains on the frayed ropes around Ben's hands were getting steadily bigger. His eyes darted around the room for escape and caught something in the mirror.

Ben thought he saw a ghost.

✳ ✳ ✳

Alisha emerged from under the bed, silent as a shadow. One guard had his back to her. She wondered how he did not hear her heartbeats thudding wildly. Alisha gripped the blade tightly in her hands. *One step more… If he turns now, I am done for.*

Alisha clasped his mouth and swiftly slashed his neck, ensuring she got the jugular vein. He convulsed, but she held him in an iron grip and let his blood spill on the floor. Alisha checked for a pulse but felt none. She laid him on top of the bed. She took a deep, calming breath and steadied her thundering heart.

Just as Alisha heard footsteps approaching the room, she quickly rushed to hide behind the door. This time, she was glad to see the gunman who was about to walk inside. She'd found her target with the reluctant face. This was the same gunman who'd cave under interrogation. *Let's see how much you talk.*

Alisha stepped out soundlessly, pulling out a syringe. She drove the needle inside the man's neck and emptied it. He turned to face her with wild, raging eyes, but his voice caught in his throat, and he slowly slumped like an unsupported mannequin. She dragged him across to the bed where the first gunman lay dead.

Alisha inhaled a deep breath and crept ahead, quickly darting into the corridor. She straightened up and listened to the other room.

"Any last words, *Yehud*?" came Abu Tawil's sneering voice.

CHAPTER 8

Alisha heard a final prayer.

Ben Shapiro's head drooped on his chest in shocked defeat. His blue eyes had a look of haunted helplessness as he murmured in ragged breaths in Hebrew, *"Hear me, oh Israel…"*

Alisha froze as she recognised the language. *This was Hebrew. The golden-haired stranger was unmistakably Jewish.* She suddenly recollected that the word '*Yehud*' meant Jew.

Alisha silently dashed ahead, drawing her blade. *I have to take my chances.* Cupping the mouth of the third gunman, she drove the blade into his neck with all her strength.

"For, our Lord, our God is one…"

Alisha moved like lightning.

Ben's words echoed faintly in her ears, as adrenaline pumped through her veins. She locked the gunman into place tightly, reached into his belt, and pulled out his gun. Alisha wrenched the blade out of his neck and laid him on the floor. Blood gushed over her shoes, staining them red. She panicked and thought in desperation, *I'm not going to make it in time.*

As Ben Shapiro closed his eyes in finality, a tear of regret ran down his cheek as he finished his last line,

"And blessed be the name of His glorious kingdom forever and ever…"

Ben's ears exploded with the sound of two gunshots as a sharp cry emerged from his throat. His eyes jerked open to see a fine mist of blood envelop him. Abu Tawil fell aside with a loud *thunk* on the floor, dead.

Ben Shapiro looked up and reeled in shock at the young woman pointing a gun straight at him.

* * *

The woman approached him swiftly, her presence commanding. She urged, "We need to leave, now." She untied him and pushed a glass of water in his trembling hands. "Who are you?" Ben gasped. She replied, "I'll answer all those questions later."

Ben sat motionless in his chair as he slowly recovered from the trauma. His blue eyes focused sharply on her. He couldn't quite place her accent – it was too crisp to guess. She glanced at him. "Did they torture you too much?"

Ben gave a weak chuckle, his voice hoarse, "Not as much as I thought they would." He noticed her scrambling around, picking all the ammunition off the dead men's bodies with unnerving efficiency. She took her time to strip and search all the bodies, carefully searching for identity cards.

The woman murmured, "My team will be here shortly. They were already supposed to reach here before." Ben's eyes suddenly became alert again. "Who are you?" he repeated. She smiled gently. "Don't be afraid. I just saved your life, you know." Ben's eyes darted to the guns, but the woman was too quick for him. She moved them out of his reach and spoke, "There's no need for that. You'll be coming with me. Don't make me force you."

The woman knelt directly in front of him and said with quiet authority, "You need medical attention. Cooperate with me, please. And please don't make me hurt you. You've already been tortured enough." Ben fell silent.

There was a knock on the door. She motioned at Ben to stay silent. Gathering all the guns, she hurried off to open the door. A few moments later, two men came into the room. The woman jerked her head towards Ben and murmured a few words in their ears.

The two men hoisted Ben up and gently helped him across the room. The woman hurried after them. She darted inside the other room where Ben could see her and another man dragging one of the gunmen who had kidnapped him. He was unconscious and they used Ben's ropes to restrain him. She used Abu Tawil's black mask to blindfold him. Her movements were methodical, almost routine. *So, they're taking him along too*, thought Ben. The woman turned to Ben with a handkerchief in her hand. With a slightly apologetic tone, she said, "I'm going to have to blindfold you, too."

Several minutes later, a dark sedan with tinted windows carrying all of them zoomed away from the building.

✳ ✳ ✳

Alisha removed the blindfold from Ben's eyes and helped him into a chair. After she'd finished examining his injuries, she opened a small wooden cabinet next to him. She unzipped a medical kit and pulled out a roll of medical gauze. She spoke, "Well, on the bright side, your injuries aren't deep." Ben replied, "I know. I've had worse." Alisha merely raised an eyebrow at him and dabbed antiseptic ointment on his battered skin. She continued, "But I think you'd better get yourself checked at a hospital." Ben said flatly, "No hospitals." She shrugged. "Okay, your choice."

After she'd finally stepped away from him, Ben looked around and remarked casually, "Nice safehouse. Has my kidnapper spoken anything yet?" Alisha said nothing, but her eyes narrowed at him.

Alisha pulled up a chair directly in front of him. She asked, "What's your name?" After a long silence, Ben replied quietly, "Raphael."

Alisha continued, "Why are you tailing Soumik Chandra?" Ben blinked. "Who?" Alisha snapped, her patience wearing thin, "Are we really playing this game?" He responded earnestly, "Look, I really don't know who this guy is. Now, I've answered all your questions, let me go."

Alisha shook her head. "I'm not letting you go until I'm satisfied." She stalked off and gestured at one of her team members to watch Ben. He rolled his eyes at her in clear irritation.

Alisha picked up the secure line and spoke into the phone. Radhika Menon answered the call. She narrated the entire ordeal that had taken place. Alisha murmured, "... I don't know. He said his name was Raphael. I thought at first that he's from a very elite drug cartel. But he's Jewish, so I'm guessing that he might just be registered in the Israeli government's database. We took one of the gunmen from Abu Tawil's gang. He might be from the terror organisation, Hizb-Ut-Tahrir. I'll interrogate him when he wakes up."

Radhika Menon's voice came crisply, "Abu Tawil was definitely part of the Hizb-Ut-Tahrir group sometime before. And this is a legacy terror organisation that has footprints in around 50 countries across the world. They were founded in Jerusalem in the 1950s, so they would certainly have an edge there. Maybe he was secretly working with both, Hamas *and* Hizb-Ut-Tahrir to resolve their political differences.

One of your team members just sent me Raphael's photo. I'm trying to get an ID on him from my Israeli counterpart. Don't let him go till then. Give me an hour. If this involves Abu Tawil and anyone registered with the Israeli government, then I need to arrange an urgent meeting. And make sure you get everything out of Abu Tawil's gang member."

Ravi Pathak was also on the phone. He chimed in, "My team is still searching for the assassins who killed our scientists. If this gang member gives any indication that he has any knowledge about it, then get it from him. Even if it means *completely* breaking him." Alisha replied, "Got it," determination hardening her features.

She set the phone down and headed back to Ben. Alisha smirked slightly and asked good-humouredly, "While we're waiting, would you like some hummus and pita?" Ben turned his penetrating blue gaze towards her. She instinctively felt that this man was adept at reading minds. He asked, "What's your name?"

Alisha replied without hesitation, "Makhtoom."

Despite his pain, Ben chuckled softly. "You need to be a *much* better liar than *that* when you're working for any government, *Makhtoom.*"

✳ ✳ ✳

Radhika Menon frowned at the reports coming in from the Israeli desk. As she read the report, her brows furrowed deeper and deeper. *What the hell was going on?*

Menon clamped the files under her arm and walked briskly towards the secure line to place a phone call. She sat in the chair and pulled a notepad towards her. Her small hand flew across the notepaper as the questions poured out of her mind.

Trivedi lowered the receiver and said quietly, "Israel is ready for you, ma'am." Menon adjusted her headset and said pleasantly, "Good afternoon and Shalom."

Half an hour later, she hung up the phone call. She stared at the phone, still processing everything she'd heard and slowly raised her eyes to meet Ravi Pathak's alert brown ones.

Menon dialled the secure line to Alisha. "Your hunch paid off. Raphael is from the Israeli government, alright. In fact, he's from the Mossad. They were not ready to confirm him at first, but now they understand the situation. He's not an ordinary operative. The Sayeret Matkal will be coming to pick him up at a certain location."

After she'd finished the call with Alisha, Menon sat drumming her fingers on the table. *There was very little time and a lot of decisions to make.*

* * *

Nael Fakhouri, the gunman whom Alisha had knocked unconscious now stared up at her in fear, bound and broken as she towered over him. He shuddered as waves of pain coursed through his body. He'd been tied up and he realised that his gun was missing. *Where was his superior, Abu Tawil and his brothers?* Alisha looked at him coldly and asked yet again, "Why do you want Soumik Chandra?" Nael could not take the pain anymore. But he could not afford to give up any names either.

Alisha stood over him and said softly, "Alright. I'll change the question. Who else was in that meeting in Hotel Divan?" Nael still did not reply, his lips pressed tightly together. Alisha tilted her head slightly and waited for him to talk. He finally raised his head and spat at her. It was as though something inside her snapped. She raised her hand and slapped him hard across the face, right under his eye. Cold fury burst through her, and she reached for the pliers from the table. She grasped his fingernail with the pliers and yanked off his index finger clean. Nael screeched with pain as blood blossomed over his flesh.

Alisha leaned in close and snarled, "After this finger, there are nine more for me to rip off from your hands. Spit on me again, and I'll include your feet to make it nineteen." Nael looked up at her through his pain and sobbed, "Please don't." Alisha moved the pliers to his next finger. Nael's eyes bugged as he stared at it in horror. "No, please, I'll talk…"

He gasped, "We-we were supposed to guard two prospective nuclear arms dealers along with Abu Tawil. They had arrived f-from Qatar and Switzerland. Istanbul is a relatively safer place to meet. Tawil was their middleman. They were interested in taking Chandra to either Iran or to the Gulf." Alisha's eyes narrowed. "And what were their names?" Nael shuddered.

She raised the pliers again. Nael beseeched her with his eyes. "Please, no-no. I will tell you. It was a-a small-time diamond trader – Suresh Thandan. And the-the other one was Al-Jabari." Alisha frowned, "Al-Jabari… do you mean Khaled Mohammed al-Jabari?" Nael nodded weakly, staring at the floor. "We th-then saw the *Yehud* following us. The Iranians tipped us off that someone would be tailing us." Alisha frowned, "But you're from the Hamas."

Nael sneered, "So? Iran finances both, the Hamas *and* the Hezbollah. We don't like the Hezbollah, but Abu Tawil is a visionary. He said that we must build a better arsenal of weapons if we want to fight against Israel." He looked up at her and grimaced, "And now, we have the finances for it." She murmured, "And did Abu Tawil command members of the Hamas to kill scientists anywhere abroad?" Nael looked confused, "What?" Alisha repeated the question, but he continued to frown in confusion. She realised, *he doesn't know. The assassins who killed our scientists were local to India.*

Alisha's expression hardened as she asked, "And how does Soumik Chandra fit here?" Nael replied, "The Iranians were interested in working with Chandra on their nuclear project.

But why don't you ask him instead? Couldn't find him, could you?" He looked at her in a sneer and bared his teeth.

Alisha struck the pliers across his face, leaving a fresh gash. Nael's head drooped to his chest. Alisha stood there for a few moments and then strode out. She dialled Radhika Menon and spoke, "I'm sending you the recordings of the interrogation. Listen to this. I'll hold on."

After Menon had finished listening to the interrogation, she spoke, "Khaled Mohammed al-Jabari is the head of Hamas's Qatar branch. So, he met Chandra?" Alisha responded, "Yes." Menon continued, "Well, Chandra's story isn't quite fitting in here… Now listen to me very carefully. There's going to be a change in our plans. You might need to take a small detour. I'm going to send a clean-up crew to wipe off all the evidence wherever you've been, so nothing can tie you back to any possible investigations. And now, you need to do *exactly* as I say…"

Radhika Menon rushed off to meet the Joint Secretary of the Research and Analysis Wing in the other building, dragging Pathak with her. Considering the circumstances, it was going to be a long meeting.

Alisha walked over to Ben Shapiro who was scraping dried blood off his knees. She tossed the pliers in his hands, jerked her head towards Nael, and murmured, "He's all yours."

* * *

Anil Roy, the Joint Secretary of the R&AW, let out a long sigh as he took his glasses off and stared out of the window. The soft glow of Delhi's skyline did little to lighten the weight on his shoulders. Radhika Menon had just finished briefing him and she finally took a deep breath, her tone crisp and her tension evident. Ravi Pathak sat beside her, arms crossed, his face a grim mask of worry.

As Roy polished his glasses with his shirt, he spoke, his voice tinged with exhaustion, "On days like these, Radhika… I sometimes wonder why I haven't retired yet." The corners of Menon's mouth turned upwards. She replied, "We'd all retire sir, but someone has to clean up the mess. Till when can we get an approval for this new mission, sir?" He sighed, "We have great strategic relations with Iran since many years, Radhika. And we cannot afford to compromise those, especially the Chabahar Port. But we can't hand over our nuclear scientists to them, either. We still don't know who's behind the killings of our scientists yet, do we?" Menon and Pathak shook their heads.

Roy picked up his secure line, his frustration simmering and spoke, "Get the National Security Advisor on the line. We need to arrange a very urgent meeting."

As Radhika Menon left his office, she glanced at Pathak already rushing ahead of her. She couldn't help thinking… *Alisha Nair is going to need plenty of luck for this one. There was too much at stake now.*

* * *

The phone rang insistently at the bedside of the Deputy Director of the Mossad, Yaakov Cohen. Startled, he awoke with a jerk and threw his blankets off. He picked up the receiver and confirmed his identity. A voice spoke, "Your presence is requested at the office immediately. The car is waiting."

Scrambling around for a fresh shirt, Yaakov Cohen glanced at his wristwatch. It was 2 am. Cohen wondered which emergency it was this time.

* * *

Half an hour later, Deputy Director Yaakov Cohen was sitting beside Katriel Levy, the room heavy with tension. A few top members of the Sayeret Matkal as well as the Defence Minister also sat opposite them, watching him intently.

They stared at the desk phone in the middle of the polished conference table. A voice spoke, "Connecting you to the Joint Secretary of the Research and Analysis Wing of India, Anil Roy."

Moments later, a voice spoke warmly, "Shalom, Mr. Cohen. I apologise for the lateness of the hour. But this could not wait."

Yaakov Cohen leaned forward and replied, "We understand the situation, sir. Have you been briefed by our government about the recent incidents?" Roy replied in the affirmative.

Cohen continued, "Our interest lies in taking down Khaled Mohammed al-Jabari, the head of the Hamas's Qatar branch. We have received information that he will be in Palestine soon." Roy responded, "And our main interest is getting back Soumik Chandra *alive*. Khaled Al-Jabari was in fact, connected to financing one of the blasts that had happened in India. Our assets in Istanbul and Tel Aviv are already coordinating with each other."

Cohen gave a curt nod and said, "I assure you that we will extend our help and any services to them. The mission however…" he hesitated and chose his words carefully, "is more challenging than we anticipated. We do not know how many identities of our assets have been leaked to Khaled Al-Jabari at the moment."

The voice of the Indian National Security Advisor came in, "Mr. Cohen, we anticipated the same. I have a suggestion here." He gave a slight cough. "Why don't our assets take down *your* targets, and your assets could take down *ours*? That way, we reduce the chances of exposure on both sides." There was a long silence.

Cohen raised his eyes to his peers sitting around him. Katriel Levy looked doubtful, but the members of the Sayeret Matkal nodded. Cohen's eyes swept over each face, and he made a decision.

"We're giving the go ahead for this. But please share the recordings of the interrogations of every target with us. We'll send you the tapes from our side, as well. Our assets will be informed, and the next plan of action will be decided."

Anil Roy spoke, "Alright. Thank you for your cooperation, Mr. Cohen. Our assets will coordinate with yours and then take it forward from there. All the best, sir." Yaakov Cohen said quietly, "And to you, sir."

Sitting across Anil Roy, Ravi Pathak closed his eyes and breathed a prayer for Alisha. As he finished it, his bushy brows creased slightly as he thought, *good luck, darling. I'll be watching you from afar...*

CHAPTER 9

Back in India, the silver-haired gentleman pressed the tips of his fingers together as he glanced up at the skies, deep in thought. He was known by many codenames over the years; MR-9, TAR-57, Sahir, or Dhruv. However, he seemed to prefer the codename 'Dhruv' the most. It was a rather fitting name for the retired ex-Joint Secretary of the R&AW who once belonged to the office of special operations.

Each game I play is a complex battle, he mused. As he slowly lowered his gaze, his shrewd eyes lingered on the beautiful yellow and pink flower shrubs. Right next to his elbow, snacks were neatly arranged in blue ceramic dishes on a small food trolley. Still in deep contemplation, he now gazed at the tomato cheese sandwiches, biscuits, and hot coffee. A large brown paper envelope was wedged between the dishes. *So, the higher powers have finally answered my calls*, he thought with a faint smirk. However, as he sat on the garden-facing porch of his luxurious villa, he simply wanted to relax in that very moment. And yet, he could not put his mind at ease because of his turbulent thoughts. He briefly closed his eyes and sighed.

There were too many who have suffered, and I have the power to change things. With a sigh, he grasped the armrests of his rocking chair and reluctantly pushed himself out of it. He let his bare feet absorb the coolness of the freshly watered grass. It was incredible how much joy such simple things gave. The hardened soles of his feet felt strangely sensitive in the grass. Was this a tell-tale sign of a retired, luxurious life in his past few years?

But my journey has been far from luxurious, he thought darkly. How many times had he cheated death? How many times had he felt like screaming in frustration almost every other day in his younger years? Yet, he had relentlessly carried on. The life of a diplomat had a very different kind of turbulence; the kind that common citizens never even dreamt of. Especially, those diplomats who took their job seriously. Even retired diplomats like him, who put their life on the line.

He sighed once again, strode back towards his armchair, and picked up the brown paper envelope. As he settled comfortably in his armchair, he quickly glanced around, even though he knew there was no one around to disturb him or snoop on him. *Force of habit*, he concurred. He opened the envelope and reached inside to pull out a confidential brown file. He laid it on the trolley beside the dishes and smoothened out its yellowed, wrinkled corner. *This is going to hurt.* He opened the file which also contained a photo. His eyes fell upon the prominent name printed at the very top. *Prakash Kamat.* He had pulled in a lot of favours to get this.

He finally reached out for a sandwich and bit into it, as distant memories of his past flooded his mind. *A gross injustice had occurred decades ago… And it was time to make it right. If I didn't, then more lives would be destroyed.*

He leant back in his chair and frowned as he stared into space. He knew that he would be risking everything. *And for what?* He wondered. *I am officially retired. My life finally deserves some peace in my twilight years.* He opened the file and stared at the faded photograph. He sipped his coffee slowly, turbulent thoughts crashing in his mind. Deep down, he already knew the answer. He gave a slight sigh and finished his coffee.

Unofficially, spies never retired.

✳ ✳ ✳

Ravi Pathak frowned at the article that had just caught his eye, *'EcoCare NGO protests against the development of a nuclear project in Andhra Pradesh.'* He stared at the name of the NGO, 'EcoCare'. *Protesting against a nuclear project?* As far as he knew that region had only obtained government clearance as of now, and it was a completely legal move. *How had the NGO got to know of this?* Pathak flung the newspaper aside, pondering over what he'd just read. *The name sounded familiar... Where have I heard of that name before?* Suddenly, it clicked. *Wasn't this NGO banned for having Naxalite links?* Pathak pulled out a drawer and reached for a file. He opened it and began riffling through its pages. *And there...* His index finger stopped at the name, and he cursed out loud. *These bloody Naxalites were worse than Jihadis.*

EcoCare was funded by a particularly sinister foundation that had links to foreign intelligence agencies. Pathak was sure that these protests had nothing to do with saving the environment. They were only doing it to draw international attention to the nuclear project and stop its construction. He dialled a number and spoke authoritatively, "Conduct a raid on the office of the NGO 'EcoCare'. They had already been banned some time back, so they're not allowed to conduct any protests. Arrest their head and freeze their accounts. And make them confess who paid them to protest against the development of that nuclear facility." Pathak slammed down the phone and heaved a sigh of exasperation.

Pathak wondered how many subsidiaries and back-end joints of foreign agencies he could stop in his lifetime. He thought about the bigwigs like the Ford Foundation that had western funding for anti-India activities. Thousands of NGOs in India were funded by such foundations that had headquarters in the west or in the Gulf. Some NGOs were also funded by the Vatican. And all of them were always connected to several deep state organisations.

His mind wandered over to Alisha and the meeting with the Deputy Director of the Mossad. Pathak wished he were there to protect and assist her with the mission, but he couldn't trust anyone else with his current investigation of the murders of nuclear scientists. As a father, he was terrified for his little girl. And as her primary handler and trainer, he was confident that she could handle it smoothly. *It was remarkable how human emotions could push someone into such deep anxiety and absolute certainty all at once,* he thought.

He hoped that the Mossad would protect her well. Pathak had a long experience of knowing only too well that anything could go sideways within just a few seconds during a mission. Sometimes, even crucial missions could get cancelled. Decades ago, a covert Indian operation that planned the bombing of Pakistan's nuclear reactor under construction at Kahuta got cancelled. Israel had offered to bomb the plant, considering they had a common enemy in Pakistan back then. A Pakistani spy had even mentioned that the Pakistani government had also planned a preemptive strike on India. Pathak closed his eyes and shook his head at the monstrous mistakes that the then-Prime Minister, Morarji Desai had committed. In a friendly conversation over the phone, Desai had told Pakistan's General Zia-ul-Haq that he knew about their plans of constructing a nuclear plant at Kahuta. *How could a Prime Minister sell out his own nation?*

The planned covert mission had become a diplomatic and security disaster. The ISI had rounded up more than 200 R&AW agents working in Pakistan, and brutally tortured and massacred all of them. The fallout had been catastrophic. There was also immense international pressure on India from Washington to stop the covert mission. And finally, despite so many officers trying to stop the inevitable, Pakistan had managed to become a nuclear power. The deepest level of shame was, Morarji Desai was honoured with the highest civilian award of Pakistan, the *Nishan-e-Pakistan*.

And if anything happened to Alisha... Pathak firmly drove the horrible thoughts out of his mind. *She could at least be exfiltrated from there.* He gave a wry smile. He was glad that India had relatively good relations with both, Israel and Palestine.

But Pathak had much more faith in this mission, its people, and the current Indian Prime Minister. He knew that every government had deep faults, but at least the current Prime Minister took India's national security very seriously. Even the IB's work had increased and terror attacks had subsequently reduced. However, he wondered how many officers had been put to scrutinise the movements of political figures from the opposition party. *But that's how all governments work...*

Pathak closed the file and threw it back into the drawer, shaking his head. No matter how hard an intelligence officer worked, there was always something that slipped past.

* * *

The man called Knight looked down in triumph. He climaxed as the girl arched her back under him. He let go with a groan, as she fell back into his bed, panting. As he collapsed on top of her, she smirked at him and asked, "Another round?" Knight wondered, *good lord, did she not get tired already?*

An hour later, Knight glanced at the girl sleeping soundly in his bed. He headed out into his balcony and gazed up at the stars twinkling down at the bustling city. *I have changed so much since I left home...* The distant hum of traffic barely reached his ears as Knight lit a cigarette and took a long drag. He watched the tiny swirls of grey smoke drifting lazily up towards the sky.

He ignored the snores of the girl sprawled in his bed. Her smooth, satin undergarments lay strewn all over the floor. She had dragged a blanket over her nude body, one arm draped lazily over the edge. Knight turned back to stare at the city below him, but he was lost in the memories of his childhood. He closed his eyes and tried to drown the screams of his mother from his head.

Knight was suddenly back home in Gulmarg, Kashmir. He was hardly thirteen years old when he was returning from school. The backpack weighed heavy on his shoulders, as he had borrowed three extra books from the library today instead of two. He loved to read literature and had become the librarian, Mrs. Mattoo's favourite. She had secretly allowed him to take one more book. Mrs. Mattoo had stuffed one extra book into his hands, patted him on the head, and hurried away with a fond smile and a twinkle in her eyes. Knight had smiled after her happily. As he returned home, an Indian army soldier accosted him.

Knight smiled at them and waved. He was friendly with the soldiers. They greeted him and tossed an apple in his hands. The soldiers were snacking together on a small sack of apples. Knight thanked them and moved ahead, turning round the corner into his lane. He remembered the kind words from one of them. A few weeks ago, an Indian army captain; Yusuf Marfani, had patted Knight's shoulder, eyeing the many books he carried under his arms.

Captain Yusuf leant close to him and said proudly, "Beta, I really appreciate that you're interested in education. If you ever wish to take up guns against India for some quick money, you talk to me first, okay? You can always trust us. If anyone approaches you or troubles you to start Jihad, tell me right away. I'll keep you safe from them. They should never come between you and your education." And Knight had nodded at him enthusiastically and said, "Thank you, sir." The captain replied smiling, "Call me Captain Yusuf."

As Knight approached his house, he recognised the tall, familiar figure emerging out of the main door. It was his brother. He felt the sudden anxiety rising in his chest as the figure loped towards him with a smirk. When would his brother learn? Unlike him, his brother, Atiq had never been interested in academics. The brothers had a warm relationship, but it had recently come under tremendous strain because of Atiq's behaviour. Atiq had turned to Jihad because it was a quicker way of earning money. The ISI and Kashmiri separatists paid quick money to stone pelters and information suppliers.

"Got friendly with those Indian dogs again, did you?" spat Atiq. Knight averted his eyes and tried to rush inside the house, but Atiq blocked his path. He grabbed Knight's head and forced him look straight into his eyes. "Listen to me, little brother. Those books aren't going to take you anywhere. Look at me – I'm already helping our cause." Knight told him defiantly, "And what cause is that, Atiq? I'm not going to do anything that will upset Ammi." Atiq snarled, "You'd better not go and join those Indian bastards, brother. I'm already helping the cause in ways that you can never imagine. Tonight is going to be a big night for us. So, stay out of my way, and don't tell Ammi."

He hurried away, leaving Knight staring after him. Atiq's words rang in his ears. 'Tonight is going to be a big night for us...' Knight was anxious. What was Atiq up to now? What if he ruined everything for their family? Surely, Atiq just needed some convincing. He ran after Atiq and watched him turn around the corner. Knight followed him silently. Where was he going? What was he planning?

It was getting late. Ammi was going to wonder where her boys were. Six lanes away, Atiq finally slowed and disappeared into a house. Knight wondered whose house this was. Not daring to breathe, Knight hesitantly followed and crouched by the window, peeking inside. There seemed to be several people moving in the dimly lit room. A deep voice spoke, "… We have much to do, and all of us have received our instructions. Well done, Atiq bhai. Tonight, we'll have some fun with all of them. And leave that pretty Mattoo whore to me… I have some special plans for her." He heard raucous laughter at the words. Horrified, he saw the silhouette of several guns against the curtain.

Surely, they did not mean Mrs. Mattoo, the librarian? The Mattoo family was one of the last few Pandit families that had still bravely remained in this area. All their Pandit neighbours had fled to Srinagar after Knight's family friends had brutally murdered the elder Pandits and driven out their entire families. He hadn't liked what had happened to those Pandits, but he'd also never spoken against their murders. However, to him, Mrs. Mattoo was different. After all, she was his favourite teacher.

Knight's stomach churned. He had heard enough. Quietly, he crept out of the gate and sprinted up the lane. His heart hammered as the words echoed in his ears. He was sickened at how they'd spoken about Mrs. Mattoo. Anguish filled him as he wondered what Atiq had done. Knight was determined to stop him before something bad happened. Mrs. Mattoo had always very been kind to him. In fact, she'd taught him extra lessons when he had requested her. Panic filled him and he ran as hard as he could. 'I can't tell Ammi anything either… What shall I do now?', he wondered with desperation.

As he rounded one of the last few lanes, he ran straight into someone and lost his balance. He cried out as he fell hard on the ground. Pain exploded in his knee as he clutched at it tightly. "Oh no, I'm so sorry-" exclaimed a voice he recognised well. Knight looked up to see Captain Yusuf reaching down for him. Strong arms grasped Knight and hauled him back to his feet.

"So sorry, beta. Let me look at that knee. And… what has happened to you?" Captain Yusuf's alarmed voice pulled Knight out of his panic. Knight cried out, "My-my brother Atiq. They got him,

sir. Please help me... They're going to kill the Mattoo family tonight." Captain Yusuf's expression shifted instantly, his eyes sharp and alert as he asked, "Are you sure, boy?" Knight panted, "Yes, I heard them discussing what they were going to do to them. Please, please help Atiq. He doesn't know what he's doing." Captain Yusuf smoothly picked him up, slung him across his thick shoulders, and ran all the way to the small group of soldiers patrolling in the main street.

They stared as Captain Yusuf climbed into a van and gently laid Knight in the back. As he dabbed a swab of medicine on Knight's bloodied knee, he ordered, "Tell me everything you heard." The other soldiers had now assembled around them.

Through shaky breaths, Knight narrated everything that had happened. Captain Yusuf turned and spoke grimly to his subordinates, "You heard the boy. Alert the other units and ask them to reach the residence of the Mattoo family immediately. Gather extra ammunition, boys." Knight begged him, "Please, sir... Please I beg you not to hurt Atiq. He is my brother."

Captain Yusuf said gently, "We won't. Thank you, my boy. You might just save several lives tonight. We'll drop you back home on our way." Knight protested, but the captain was firm. "No, I don't want you to get hurt in all this mess," he said, strapping on his bullet-proof vest across his enormous chest. Walkie-talkies buzzed as the van roared to life and lurched off.

Several minutes later, Knight was back home. He watched through his window as the van full of soldiers sped away. Knight waited in agony. He couldn't stand it... He had to know what was happening. Despite his injured knee, he limped all the way in the cold weather to the Mattoo residence. When he finally arrived, he stared around in disbelief. Why was everything silent? He decided to wait and dived into the shrubs.

About half an hour later, a small car arrived. Atiq and a few other people stepped out. They all carried guns. Knight recognised their faces – they were all wanted by the Indian government. He watched in silence as they knocked on the beautiful teakwood door of the Mattoos' residence. Atiq's eyes narrowed in glee as he loaded his gun. And suddenly, shouts filled the air. Knight turned to see Captain Yusuf and his soldiers surround them all. The older gunmen raised their Kalashnikovs to fire, but the soldiers had already started shooting right at them.

Knight watched in horror as Atiq aimed his gun at the nearest soldier. But before he'd pulled the trigger, a volley of bullets had blasted Atiq backwards, drowning Captain Yusuf's shouts of, "No, don't shoot-" Knight screamed as he watched his brother fall, blood spurting out in torrents from several bullet wounds. He heard Captain Yusuf shout incomprehensible words, but he ran forward and cradled his brother's lifeless body in his arms. "No-no... Atiq," he sobbed. "It's all my fault."

He felt a powerful hand on his shoulder and turned around to see Captain Yusuf's grim face. "I'm sorry, beta." And from that very moment, a deep hatred seared Knight's stomach like acidic bile at the very sight of all those soldiers in olive-green uniforms. His brother lay dead in front of him, murdered by these very people who'd promised him that they would protect him and his family.

The shocked faces of the Mattoo family surrounded him. He felt a sudden weight lifted off his shoulder and looked up through his tears. Mrs. Mattoo had taken off his backpack that was now soaked in Atiq's blood. Tears rolled down her rosy cheeks and she covered her mouth with shaking hands. He stared at her with accusing eyes. It was all her fault, she was the target, not his brother... "You should've died... It should've been you, not Atiq," he screamed at her hoarsely.

He watched her face slowly change from anguish to fury, but looking at his brother's empty eyes, he felt no remorse. She slapped him hard across the face, regretting it instantly. But before he could retaliate, the soldiers pinned his arms behind his back.

Later in the night, when Atiq's body had arrived home, Ammi's wails had echoed throughout the night. Even after the funeral, Captain Yusuf had stayed with them as a plain-clothes security officer, helping out with anything they needed. The soldiers interrogated them thoroughly. When Captain Yusuf had spoken privately to Ammi, Knight had watched him with undisguised hatred. To him, they could've done anything to save Atiq. Instead, they'd murdered him in cold blood.

Captain Yusuf had approached him, but Knight had turned away in disgust. He seized Knight by the shoulders and said sincerely, "Beta, I'm sorry for what happened. I cannot get your brother back, but we will fund your education and everything you need till you finish graduation. Your mother has agreed to it." Education? thought Knight in fury. Which book had saved Atiq on that fateful night? Knight sneered, "Save your filthy government's money. I don't need it. You killed my brother."

Captain Yusuf looked at him gravely and spoke, "You'll move on from this trauma, boy. I hope you do. Your brother was wrong to raise that gun and even a sensible boy like you knows it deep down. No child should even hold a gun in the first place. Like you, he should've learned to hold a book instead." Knight looked away, tears spilling out of his eyes.

The captain continued gently, "Maybe one day, beta… One day you'll understand the brutal nature of our jobs and why we have to do all this. Sometimes, we have no choice but to shoot. I hope you understand everything one day." With a heavy sigh, Yusuf placed a hand on his shoulder and walked away. Knight stared after him, teeth bared, wishing he could slit the captain's throat and rejoice in *the blood gushing out of him. It was as though a bandage had been removed from his eyes. They were all the same...*

Two months later, he'd received a strange request. A note had arrived at his home, requesting him to join Atiq's cause. He'd quickly hidden it from Ammi and had avoided her eyes during dinner. She had immediately sensed his discomfort. Later that night, Ammi had tucked him in bed. Knight had pretended to be asleep, but she brushed his hair and turned his face around.

She sighed and said sternly, "Don't follow your brother, Faisal. Even you know that he was wrong. We love him and we miss him, but you cannot continue what he did. I-I can't lose my second son," she begged him, her plea raw and desperate. Knight sat up and gave her a hug. They'd sobbed together for several hours, and Ammi had finally fallen asleep at dawn, still cradling him.

However, Knight lay awake. One day... One day he would avenge Atiq. He swore to himself. Although Ammi had forced him to make peace with what had happened, Knight had never forgiven or forgotten. She was so proud when he had gained that scholarship to that university in America. She had underestimated him. He'd carried that note all the way to America and had only shown it to Professor Farooqi.

And when Professor Farooqi had guided him to the path of light, it had been so simple and yet so illuminating. He had encouraged Knight to submit articles to his friends who worked at the New York Times and the Washington Post, and even offered to review them for him. He had carefully chosen to leave out the part where Atiq had raised his gun first, prepared to shoot the soldier or the fact that Atiq fully intended to kill the Mattoo family.

Knight had simply moulded the narrative to make it sound like the soldiers had gunned down four misguided Kashmiri civilians. There was also no mention of how they had conspired to massacre and rape the Mattoo family, similar to what Atiq's friends had done to more than hundred thousand of other such Kashmiri Pandit families.

His first article, 'The true face of the Indian army in Kashmir – a helpless Kashmiri youth speaks…' was crafted with precision and deceit. It was well-received by the audience. The overwhelming response at his article made him even more determined to write several more. He realised that as a first-hand Kashmiri youth, there were many takers for his articles in the media.

And thus, he had chosen to call himself 'Knight' and avenge all his fallen brothers. Years and years of pent-up hatred had suddenly gushed out in ugly torrents like a burst dam. They'd killed his brother… Now it was his turn to kill them. He had sworn to do everything he could against the Indian government.

Knight gave a cold smile as he came back to the present. His cigarette had nearly burnt out and he flicked it from the balcony, watching the ember vanish into the city below. He turned around, strolled back to his bed, and pulled the blankets comfortably around himself.

Knight decided to have a long sleep before he played the final round of his deadly cards.

* * *

"There's something wrong. Are you *sure* the results from the forensics lab are correct?" asked Pathak, staring at the lab's report in disbelief. Jay nodded and spoke grimly, "Yes sir." Pathak shuffled through the papers, trying to search for any other name in there, but the answer was clear. He slowly gazed up at Jay, eyes wide. "You do realise that this would be a very serious accusation, Jay?" said Pathak quietly.

Jay took a deep breath and replied, "Sir, this isn't an accusation, it is a confirmation of evidence. We found the fingerprints at not only one, but at *three* other crime scenes. These fingerprints were confirmed to be present at the homes of some of the victims. They're verified, alright." Pathak was silent for a while, his mind racing. He spoke after much contemplation, "*Three* crime scenes? Isn't this too… obvious?" Jay agreed, "Yes, it is, sir. But for now, this is the only evidence we have." Pathak fell silent again, processing the information.

Then, with a heavy sigh, he spoke, "Fine. Let's bring the director into custody for questioning. But make sure that this doesn't get leaked into the media, or else this will become a public spectacle."

＊＊＊

Director Vasant Prabhu of the Department of Atomic Energy glanced up from the clipboard as he finished signing his approval on the stack of administrative paperwork in front of him. "Thanks, Neelam," he said warmly, nodding gratefully at the administrator as he handed the papers over. "I don't know what I'd do without you with so much administrative paperwork on my desk." Neelam Kumari smiled back.

"Also, could you please set up a meeting with Director Sengupta, from the Atomic Minerals section? We need to go over some points and I'd like you to take some notes for the administrative procedures for some projects." She nodded. He spoke again, "Let's make sure we-" but he trailed off. Director Prabhu was staring past her at the door. Ravi Pathak stood outside the door with a steely expression, flanked by Jay and Gopal on either side. Neelam Kumari's eyes widened and darted back to Director Prabhu. Pathak held the door open for Jay and Gopal to scurry inside. He turned to Neelam and said, "We need a word in private with the director." Neelam's smile vanished and she hurried off, clutching the documents carefully.

Pathak swiftly glanced up the corridor of the director's office and quickly stepped in, closing the door behind him firmly. Director Prabhu faced him listlessly and threw up his hands as he asked, "So? Any leads, Ravi?"

Pathak merely tilted his head and asked him, "You tell me, Prabhu." Director Prabhu frowned at him, "What do you mean by-" But Jay interrupted, his tone sharp, "We found your fingerprints at three crime scenes, sir. Would you like to tell us how they got there?" Director Prabhu stared at Pathak and replied, "What the hell? Ravi, you know I wouldn't-" Pathak sighed wearily as he spoke, "And yet the fingerprints were there. You were one of the only few people who knew about Operation Anushakti directly from the Prime Minister."

Prabhu's chair screeched as he stood, his fists clenched. He snapped, "How *dare* you accuse me of betraying my country, Pathak?" Pathak replied firmly, "We're taking you in for questioning based upon some very real evidence. Let the law and the agency decide if you're guilty, Prabhu. Now, let's not make a scene out of this... I'd prefer to keep this quiet."

Director Prabhu snarled as he stormed towards the door, "I can't believe this... I thought you were better than this, Pathak. I trusted you."

Pathak watched silently as Prabhu left, his steps heavy with indignation. Closing the door behind him, Pathak couldn't help but sigh. *Was this truly over?* He wondered where the other players were and what moves were they planning.

More than a thousand kilometers away in Delhi, the Prime Minister received the news that Director Vasant Prabhu of the DAE was brought in for questioning. After his surprise and fury had abated, the Prime Minister slammed down the phone and sighed, wondering whom he could truly trust.

* * *

The nuclear research exchange student, Anya, wondered if she were doing the right thing. Her fling with the cherub-faced Middle Eastern student, Behzad had peaked an unexpected curiosity within her. *Who was this boy? Why did he never talk about his family?* Previously, Anya had wondered why he never mingled with the other exchange students or attended their parties. She even wondered why she was slightly obsessed with him. One evening, she decided to stalk him. Perhaps, she would surprise him.

But when Anya followed Behzad, she was stunned at what she saw. She had tailed him for a while. Behzad stood outside a house, watching the man inside. She hid in the bushes, watching Behzad. *Whose house was this?* She wondered. *Why is Behzad watching him?* From the distance, Anya squinted at the name plate on the pillars of the gate. She could read the name, 'Director V Sengupta, Atomic Minerals Directorate for Exploration and Research.' She frowned. The name looked familiar. *Wasn't this the same director who had delivered a special lecture on rare earth minerals for her batch of exchange students? Was Behzad a part of another nuclear project that I didn't know about?* She wondered if she should confront him. *No, that would mean he would know that I'm stalking him,* she scolded herself.

Suddenly, Behzad turned, and Anya shrank even more within the bushes. Anya froze when she saw Behzad slip a long knife into his jacket. There was a mysterious smile on his face. It was the same look that had terrified her when she'd gazed into his charcoal-black eyes when she was intimate with him. A light sheen of sweat now appeared at her forehead. Behzad left, but Anya stayed hidden within the bushes for more than an hour. As she slowly walked home, she wondered, *did I just witness an intent to murder?*

The next few days, Anya tried to push the incident out of her mind but couldn't. *I have to inform the authorities,* she told herself and made up her mind. *What if director Sengupta was really in danger? And what shall I even say? There was no evidence.* She decided to leave an anonymous tip at the department of foreign affairs as well as the police. In their first few days of visiting India, all the students from her batch were taught how to report a crime or if they were in any danger.

Anya picked up the phone with a trembling hand and whispered, "H-Hello?" She narrated everything that she'd witnessed about Behzad. She finally placed the phone back, still feeling rather stupid.

Anya suddenly wondered, *will I be in danger, too?*

* * *

The Israeli Embassy shimmered with soft, elegant lighting and festive decorations. Tiny blue and white national flags adorned the room and a lively energy buzzed among the guests. They were celebrating a festival and had invited many important guests from across different embassies. Radhika Menon's eyes swept over the guests as she stepped inside. Soft yellow light cascaded over the room and added a warm glow around the wooden portraits hung on the walls. Menon could hear bouts of laughter and conversations over the gentle clink of glasses, filled with sparkling gold champagne. Although Menon was now used to it, she still felt the familiar rush of institutional power as she strolled inside.

There was an unmistakable aura of power, secrecy, and privileged government authority inside the embassy, and it seemed to emanate from the smiling men and women in the room. They were a mixture of policy makers, undercover operatives, military generals, diplomats, consular generals, and ambassadors.

But Menon ignored that aura. *After all, what remained of a person when they were stripped off their power? Without their power, there could be a deep impact on their psychology and could possibly change their personality traits.* That psychology interested her more. *Would they associate their identity and existence with power or their position? Or could they do without it? Give a man a mask, and he shows his true face.*

Her eyes lingered on every individual, and she wondered what mask each person wore. Her gaze stopped at a familiar face smiling slightly at her from the far end of the room. Menon dropped her gaze and discreetly made her way towards the man. She accepted a glass of water from a server on the way. The man drew up a chair next to him and she casually settled into it. "Thanks for coming Eli," she murmured. Eli did not reply and simply swirled the champagne in his glass.

Menon asked lightly, "How are things at the American Consulate?" They'd known each other for several years. Eli was an American Jew who divided his time between the American embassy and the American consulate. He sipped on his champagne thoughtfully and replied quietly, "Just as they are." Menon rolled her eyes and muttered, "What, still rejecting visas of Indian students? Or is it H1B work visas this time?" Eli sighed in exasperation.

Menon leant over and asked him softly, "What do you have for me?" Eli shook his head and smiled at her. "Nothing." Menon looked at him, incensed. "Then, why did you-" But he cut her off, "You wanted some answers. And they're all there." Menon spoke slowly, trying to keep the anger out of her voice, "I told you; I want to know who's behind all this."

Eli took her hand and got to his feet, pulling her upwards. He said warmly, "It was great to see you too, Radhika." His tall frame bent down to give her a brief hug. As he did so, he whispered urgently in her ear, "It's the same people as last time."

Menon stiffened and a faint crease appeared between her eyebrows. She said blankly, "What? I don't understand who-" But he gently squeezed her hand and said, "You will, soon. *They're already watching you, Radhika.* And if I'm not careful, they'll watch me, too. I'll send you some help later. Take care." Eli turned away from her, but she held on to him and reached out for his glass. She said sweetly, "I think you need a refill."

And in the same breath, she hissed, barely moving her lips, "Who told you?" He locked his eyes on her, raised his empty glass in a mocking toast, and said smilingly, "Here's to your safety. From a friend who knows you."

Cryptic undercover bastards, thought Menon as she stared after him, frowning. *I'm being watched? Surely, he didn't mean...* She pondered over his words as he disappeared out of sight.

CHAPTER 10

In a remote street in Istanbul, a large van labelled 'Nora's Bakes' was parked next to an old hotel. Passersby hardly glanced at the faded pictures of baguettes and desserts painted on its sides. An ambulance was parked right next to the van.

Nobody could guess that the odd group of men and women disguised as chefs, doctors, and tourists huddled inside the van were undercover Israeli operatives preparing for an exfiltration operation. Ben Shapiro finished wearing his bullet-proof vest and put on a smart tuxedo over it. He had concealed his golden hair with a wig paired with a brown-haired beard. The heavy framed glasses that sat on his nose drew away attention from his blue eyes.

"In and out, quickly. We have exactly half an hour to get Soumik Chandra. Remember, we need him alive. And no lingering in this place." Ben murmured. "Everyone ready? All your earpieces and communication lines set?" He scanned the faces of his team members. The Sayeret Matkal team nodded in silent understanding. "Okay, go."

The team fanned out. Two men pulled out large trolleys of sandwiches and headed off to the back entrance. The operatives disguised as tourists headed inside the hotel. A woman dressed in hospital scrubs opened the door of the ambulance and jumped into the driver's seat, ready for extraction. Ben walked slowly, carefully watching the hotel's windows. He had already placed more operatives inside, disguised as hotel staff.

He stepped inside the building and casually strolled through the lobby towards the elevators in measured steps. He took the elevator to the sixth floor. Two armed guards flanked Soumik Chandra's room. Ben whispered into his concealed microphone, "On my signal, everybody."

Ben strode towards the guards cheerfully. He was followed by two operatives pushing a room service trolley laden with exquisite desserts. A bottle of champagne was immersed in a bowl of ice, and a bouquet of roses and jasmines was perched atop the handles of the trolley. Ben approached the guards, beaming. He bowed and announced, "Today is the 50th anniversary of this hotel and we're pleased to hand over these complimentary gifts to our esteemed guests." The guard raised his hand to stop Ben, but he ignored him.

Ben pulled out the bouquet of roses and said eagerly, "But, I insist." He thrust the roses into the guard's hands, pulling out a small device from the flowers as he did so. As Ben swiftly sprayed poison into the guard's ear, he kicked the gun away from the guard. As the second guard rushed at him, Ben landed a palm-heel strike right into his solar plexus with cat-like agility and drove a hard metallic pen with an open nib right into the base of his throat. *Not this time, you bastards.* Ben coldly watched the guard convulse and sink to the floor, as an icy chill raged in his blue eyes.

Ben surveyed both gunmen now lying motionless on the floor. He nodded at the two operatives disguised as room service staff. They knocked on the door of the adjacent room and it flew open. The operatives disguised as tourists dragged the bulky gunmen inside and then swiftly closed the door behind them.

Ben straightened up and knocked on Soumik Chandra's room. The door opened an inch and a face looked up timidly. Ben gave his most reassuring smile and gesturing to the desserts, he said, "Compliments from the hotel, sir. We bring you the most delightful desserts to serve your fine palate." Chandra hesitantly opened the door and let them inside. "I hope you like the hotel, sir" said Ben as he pushed the trolley inside.

He placed a beautifully decorated chocolate mousse into Chandra's hands and bowed, "I await your feedback." Chandra's wary eyes flicked toward the door. Ben's eyes followed his gaze. He jerked his head towards the door and said lightly, "Oh, don't worry about your friends, they're having some dessert, too."

Chandra adjusted the glasses on his nose as he glanced back at Ben. He reached for the spoon and took a couple of mouthfuls of mousse, slowly relaxing as he ate. A few moments later, Chandra reeled back and slumped on the bed.

Ben watched Chandra for a moment and then pulled his eyelid back to check his pupil. *Knocked out. Thank heavens he didn't recognise me.* He smiled slightly and patted Chandra's cheek. "We always provide the best service sir," chuckled Ben in a mocking tone. Then he raised his voice and called, "Come in." His team members rushed in.

They removed all the food and extended the trolley to Chandra's height, making it look like a stretcher. They lifted Chandra and placed him on top of the trolley. Ben along with a few operatives swiftly searched the room and crammed Chandra's documents into his suitcase. Ben carefully checked all the drawers, the floorboards, and the bathroom.

When he tapped his foot against one of the floorboards, he realised that it sounded hollow. Ben wrenched it out and reached inside. As his fingers brushed something, he frowned to himself, *there's something here.* He pulled out a long, dark cannister wedged between the planks. He opened the cannister and pulled out several long rolls of what looked like… *blueprints,* he realised. Ben's eyebrows shot up when he saw the completed engineering designs of a range of ballistic missiles and other missiles currently under development. He let out a long, low whistle. He put the blueprints back inside the cannister.

Damn, Soumik Chandra stole these from a nuclear submarine? No doubt the Indians are after his blood. Ben carefully wrapped Chandra's clothes around the cannister, wedged it inside his suitcase, and quickly repacked everything inside. "Good to go? All clear?" he asked. "Yes," replied his team.

Ben pulled out a long, white sheet and covered Chandra's face. The door to the adjacent room opened, and the operatives dressed as tourists walked inside. Ben asked them, "Did you finish arranging the bodies of the guards?" They nodded in unison. Ben handed Chandra's suitcase to them. His blue eyes flashed with urgency as he murmured, "*Do not* hand this suitcase over to *anybody else* other than me, under *any* circumstances, do you understand? Now, take this and go. Guard this with your lives. I'll see you at the safehouse and take the suitcase from you there."

Ben looked at his team members who were disguised as the room service staff. "Clean up the room thoroughly, boys." He jerked his head at the doctors. "Let's go." Together, they pushed the trolley down the corridor. "Be ready," whispered Ben as the elevator doors opened.

"Emergency," roared Ben at the top of his voice, as he vigorously wheeled the stretcher into the elevator. Alarmed, the hotel guests automatically moved out of his way. The doctors checked Chandra's pulse and declared that he needed to reach the hospital as fast as possible. Ben shouted at the crowd trying to peek at the stretcher, "I'm the hotel manager and I need this lift to be cleared." The elevator doors slammed shut. Hardly a minute later, they reached the ground floor.

The small group plunged through the lobby. People gasped and the crowd parted without question for the oncoming stretcher carrying a patient. "Move out of the way, this is a medical emergency. Get me an ambulance," yelled Ben dramatically as he ran. The ambulance had already screeched to a halt at the entrance, sirens blaring. They lifted the stretcher carrying Chandra, placed him inside, and strapped him securely. The doors slammed shut and the ambulance sped away. "Right on time, Yael," said Ben appreciatively to the woman driving the ambulance. She grinned at him in the rear-view mirror and gave him a wink.

Ben Shapiro sat smiling serenely at an unconscious Soumik Chandra as the screeching ambulance sped through Istanbul.

✳ ✳ ✳

Alisha squinted at the dazzling blue Mediterranean waters gently lapping against the sparkling golden shore from her plane's window seat. She could even make out a white speedboat zooming far deep into the blues of the Mediterranean. She took deep, calming breaths even though it was a smooth landing.

Twenty minutes later, the immigration officer glanced up at Alisha. "What are you doing in Israel?" Alisha noted how her cold sea-green eyes flickered over her face. Alisha offered a bright smile, "I'm here as a tourist. I'll be travelling around Tel Aviv, Haifa, and Jerusalem." The officer nodded at her curtly, "Show me your papers." Alisha handed over a British passport with the name, 'Aleya Thomas', and a few other documents.

As the officer inspected them, Alisha went over her last conversation with Radhika Menon. She was already feeling a mix of excitement and apprehension. Menon narrated what had transpired in the meeting with R&AW's Joint Director and the Deputy Chief of the Mossad. "You'll be going to Tel Aviv. There's a joint mission that has been agreed between both countries. You're going to be a part of this mission. The Sayeret Matkal launched a massive combing operation for Soumik Chandra, headed by Raphael. Chandra will be handed over to the Indian embassy and then brought to India right away. However," Menon paused. Alisha felt a slight trepidation, as Menon continued, "After you finish your work in Israel, I'll tell you the next plan of action. Until then, good luck."

Half an hour later, Alisha Nair strode out to greet the Tel Avivian sun.

* * *

Ben Shapiro uncrossed his legs as he watched Alisha keenly. She finished reading his reports on the dreaded terrorist, Al-Jabari and glanced up. The man was also wanted by the Indian government for financing a bomb blast that had happened in India. "You know, you could've told me before who you work for. We would've saved a lot of time," said Ben, smiling slightly. As she closed the file, he asked, "*Sab theek?*"

Alisha raised an eyebrow and asked, "And from where did you learn Hindi?" Ben laughed at her. "*Really?*" She folded her arms and frowned at him. Ben shrugged and answered, "Well, when you stay in Goa and Kasol long enough, you pick up more than just the swearwords." It was Alisha's turn to smile. "So, Soumik Chandra would be leaving for India soon?" Ben nodded at her. He replied, "Yep, him and his suitcase. I found the blueprints on him. I guess he didn't have time to sell them yet. Your team will escort him back home. We'll drug him and put him on an Air India special flight. After that, he is R&AW's baggage claim."

Alisha snorted. She asked hesitantly, "So, you really didn't know about him before?" He replied, "No. We just had information that a nuclear scientist was sent to work for the Iranians after we struck at their nuclear reactor. They're still planning to expand their base, most probably to nuclear submarines. We didn't have an ID on Chandra before. Now we do." Alisha stared off into space.

"Look," said Ben as he looked at her seriously. "You don't have to agree to a mission just because your superiors told you to." Alisha said softly, "I'm up for it." Ben replied, "We only have a week until Khaled Al-Jabari arrives in Palestine. We should be able to train you enough until then."

The door opened, and Katriel Levy walked inside. "Your files look good to me, Makhtoom. But you don't *speak* Hebrew, or the Arabic dialect spoken in the West Bank – That's going to be a problem. You'll be going in as a mute girl helping at the wedding catering." Alisha replied, her lips quirked into a small smile, "I understand Arabic, even though I may not be able to speak it the way locals do. So, I'll at least understand what they're speaking." Katriel nodded and said quietly. "Train hard, Makhtoom. You're going to need it."

✳ ✳ ✳

A volleyball narrowly missed her head, and someone called out, "Sorry!"

Alisha smiled at the group of girls dressed in sports bras and shorts, playing a very intense game of volleyball. As she strolled further down the beach, she saw a group of girls in bikinis lying in the sand, with guns slung across their bare backs. Alisha looked at them with a sense of pride. *Military training for everyone. Something we need in India, too.*

Alisha bought a small bag of chips at a kiosk. As she handed 10 Shekels, the elderly man behind the counter smiled at her and asked, "Tourist?" Alisha nodded. "Where are you from?" She hesitated, but then replied, "India." A happy smile spread slowly across his face. He spoke gently, "Then, take 5 Shekels back."

"But, why?" asked Alisha, surprised. He pressed the money into her hands and said, "Discount for people from Maa India." Alisha's eyebrows shot up her forehead. "No, but why-" He interrupted her and spoke slowly, "When I finished my military training many decades ago, I came to Maa India and stayed in Kasol. I had the most peaceful time and the best food there. I met a wise *Rishi* who taught me some incredible values for life. This is my way of saying thank you." Alisha's mouth fell open in surprise. As she walked away, she felt an unexpected moisture in her eyes. *Israelis were such warm people.*

"Don't get too emotional. Not all of us are like this," chuckled a voice behind her. She spun around to see Ben grinning at her. "I could punch you," she grumbled. Ben quickly strode alongside her. She murmured, "I almost forgot that you had me under surveillance." He shrugged apologetically. Alisha spoke up, "You have a beautiful country, you know."

Ben looked at her, surprised. "Thanks. You too, I guess?" Alisha sank down into the sand, and he joined her a moment later. He told her, "A lot of Israelis go to India after their military training, Makhtoom. I spent quite some time in an ashram doing meditation. Strangely, it really helped me connect to my culture in a much better way." Alisha turned to look at him, concern etched on her face.

He said quietly, his tone somber, "Most of us here have a parent, grandparent, uncle, aunt, or someone in the family who is a Holocaust survivor. That kind of trauma takes decades to heal. Sometimes, you can't even heal them completely. My uncle still wakes up screaming in his sleep. He was a teenager when he escaped from the Dachau concentration camp."

Ben stared distantly into the blues of the Mediterranean Sea and continued, "There are many in this world who still face the after-effects of World War II even today, you see. Not everyone in Israel enjoys military training. Some can take it, some can't. Some end up needing therapy." Alisha asked, "And what's it like for you?" He replied, his jaw tightened, "I have to keep myself as fit as possible, so that when the next war comes, I'll be ready." Alisha silently noted how he used the word '*when*' instead of '*if*'.

She said quietly, "But you all don't exactly have a choice *not to*, considering your hostile neighbouring countries." Ben gave her a tight smile and agreed, "We don't." She chortled and spoke, "It's sort of the same with us." Together, they looked at the breeze casting ripples over the deep blue sea.

After a while, Ben spoke up, "We finish your training tomorrow, Makhtoom." Alisha nodded in quiet understanding and went back to gazing into the horizon.

As her fingers dipped into the white sand, Alisha made a promise to herself.

I'm going to get Raghav here to explore this beautiful country, someday.

* * *

"No, lie back down," ordered Ben. Alisha fell back onto the mat. Their hour-long sparring session still hadn't finished. "I think you can get up in three different variations here to save tactical time. In Krav Maga particularly, you get up according to your opponent's position so that your next move will be easier for you. Now pull that out-" he pointed to her right leg, "and slide it all the way back in a circular motion. Use your hands for supporting your body. Use your toes while you're getting up. This will give you more momentum. After you're up half-way, rugby-tackle me at the legs."

Alisha executed her move perfectly and Ben was flat on his back within three seconds. He looked up at her from the mat and said, "I think you can be faster than that, Makhtoom." Alisha smiled faintly. *He's elder to me by a few years, but he's already another Uncle Ravi in the making.*

"Why are you smiling?" asked Ben staring at her. "Nothing," she replied. "You just remind me of someone." Ben tilted his head questioningly as he looked at her, but then shrugged. "Alright. Let's go, we need to teach you how to kill Al-Jabari. Katriel and I have devised a method." Alisha followed Ben to a small room where Katriel was waiting for them.

"Here," said Katriel. She pointed to a glass vial mounted on a stand. "This is prussic acid, also known as hydrogen cyanide. We've specially built a poison assassination device for this mission." Ben interjected, "Yeah, such devices were developed by the KGB in the 1950s."

Katriel continued, "There will be a cylinder hidden inside a newspaper. The cylinder will contain this vial of prussic acid, a metal detonator, and a triggering device. The trigger will push the metal detonator into the glass vial. Upon impact, the vial of prussic acid will explode and vapourise to emit cyanide gas. This gas leaves no trace of the poison after it dissolves into the air, and it cannot be found in the autopsy. However, Makhtoom… you will have to take an antidote 30 minutes before the attack, in case of an accidental overspray or even a back-spray. We're also going to give you a very small camera. Do not engage until you get confirmation that it is him. And after you finish, ensure that you take a photo of his body. After you get out of there, we will evacuate you from a certain point."

Katriel then looked at her in concern. "Makhtoom, if you feel that you cannot do this at any point of time, tell me. It's okay if you don't sign up for this." Alisha was silent. After a long time, she looked back at Katriel and said quietly, "And what's plan B?" The corners of Katriel's mouth turned upwards as she held up a syringe filled with a mysterious liquid. "But this will show up in the autopsy. That's why plan A works better."

Alisha murmured, "Then, let's do plan A." Katriel nodded. "Go get some rest. You will leave for Palestine tomorrow."

✳ ✳ ✳

Hebron, Palestine

The Israeli soldier at the security checkpoint at Jerusalem glanced at the occupants of the van and gave a curt nod. She handed back their documents, and the van moved slowly over the speed bumps. After the van crossed the white barricades, it took up speed over the long, curving road. Gusts of wind occasionally scattered the brown sand lying alongside the road right into its midst.

The city had captivated her during her brief stop. Alisha had liked Jerusalem, particularly the old citadel. She had spent an hour walking down the long, winding lanes paved from stone. The walls had an unmistakable aura of ancient wisdom. *Perhaps the wisdom of King Solomon still lingers*, she thought. Alisha gazed at the Golden Temple Mount beautifully dominating the backdrop of the city. *To think that this city had been ransacked at least 50 times... and yet, it was a place of ancient power. Just like Delhi, really. Once Indraprastha, now Delhi. The place of power never changed.*

Her fingers trailed over the bullet-riddled wall of the Zion Gate. It was almost as if she was trying to reach into the past and understand the stunning culture of this city, right from its inception. *Kings David and Solomon, or even the Queen of Sheba... so many people from ancient history had walked around in this holy city...* history textbooks had not done enough justice to Jerusalem.

As the car made a final turn, Ben Shapiro glanced in the rear-view mirror and murmured, "Welcome to Palestine." He had dyed his hair brown. Sand crunched under the wheels. Alisha sneezed as clouds of dust swirled around them. They changed a car near a café in Bethlehem to blend in better.

More than an hour later, dusk had fallen and they had reached Hebron. *So many massacres had happened here*, thought Alisha with a shudder. Four Sayeret Matkal operatives greeted them at the safehouse. Ben pointed to a dark van that had pictures of wedding celebrations painted on its sides. "This is what we'll be using to drop you." He looked at Alisha in concern, "Remember our safe word, okay? If anything goes sideways, we'll evacuate you. If Al-Jabari doesn't turn up, then just move out of there. The danger zone is the one where our van cannot reach you. Till then, Al-Jabari's guards can still capture you. And remember not to draw attention from the crowd. You won't be able to do anything against a mob. You'll have me constantly listening through your earpiece." As he finished speaking, Ben gave her a hug. His deep blue eyes gazed at her. "Be safe, Makhtoom. I'll be nearby."

By late evening, Alisha started the long walk towards the house, her niqab shielding her identity. *This is just like Kashmir all over again*, she thought as she trudged along the road. As she passed by a lane, she could see an Israeli soldier playing football with Palestinian children. All of them were laughing as the soldier balanced the ball precariously on his knee and then tossed it at a delighted child, showing him some dribbling skills.

Alisha smiled. *And this is the side that the media never portrays. New York Times, BBC, and Al-Jazeera really thrived on negativity and pro-Jihad. Just like they write anti-India articles and showcase the country in a negative light. Reality was so different on the ground when you actually saw it. War-hungry businesses and Jihad had together ripped more bonds between neighbours than the actual borders.*

The cylindrical assassination device was neatly packed in a secret compartment in her shoulder bag. Alisha felt safe under her niqab. Nobody glanced in her way. She opened her bag and quickly gulped the antidote.

She reached the house decorated with lights. Music echoed from within, and she waited outside the compound, watching the wedding celebrations. She went over everything that she and Raphael had discussed. *In and out.* They were already serving the food, which meant that the rituals had already finished. Ben was expecting Al-Jabari to arrive when the crowd would start thinning.

"Do you see him anywhere?" Ben's voice came through her earpiece. "No," Alisha murmured. Ben replied, "If he doesn't turn up, we'll have to call this operation off, Makhtoom. I don't want people to start noticing you." Alisha hissed, "No." She waited.

Fifteen minutes... Now twenty... Alisha was beginning to fear that Ben was right. Her eyes flitted up and down the road in desperation. Ben's voice crackled into her ear, "Move away now, Makhtoom." Alisha sighed in defeat and turned away. Just as she'd taken a step, a dark car with tinted windows quietly pulled up the road. Alisha froze as she saw the man getting out of the car, surrounded by 4 armed guards. *Its him.* "Raphael, he's here" she hissed. "I'm going in." She hurried inside, blending seamlessly into the crowd. The happy couple had people thronging around them and nobody paid attention to Alisha. She moved to the buffet and filled up a plate. She watched as Al-Jabari greeted the couple and handed them an envelope. She waited until Al-Jabari finally took a seat and started interacting with the guests around him.

Alisha carefully balanced the plate and slowly walked towards Al-Jabari. Eyes cast down, she bowed and handed him the food. He took the plate from her, pausing to only nod at her and continued to speak to the people surrounding him. Alisha felt the suspicious eyes of his bodyguards upon her, but she turned and walked towards the buffet. She continued to serve food to other guests until Al-Jabari had finished. He got up to head towards the washroom. *Now*, Alisha thought to herself. She glanced at his bodyguards. They looked relaxed. She swiftly followed him to the washroom.

Alisha watched Al-Jabari washing his hands from behind a column. She pulled out the newspaper carefully that Katriel had given her. Just as he turned around to head back, she crossed him. Alisha thrust the newspaper into Al-Jabari's face, quickly pulled the trigger and walked away. She glanced back to see a small white gaseous cloud hover in his face for a few moments before evaporating quickly. Al-Jabari gasped and clutched his throat as he collapsed into the wall next to him. She quickly snapped a photo of his slumped body from the camera and tucked the device deep inside her shirt.

Alisha moved back to the buffet table. She watched his bodyguards from afar. So far, they hadn't noticed anything. She slipped out of the house and hurried away into the quiet street. About twenty meters away, she heard the first scream. *The body had been discovered.* Alisha broke into a run. *Where was the evacuation van?*

Just then, Ben's voice cackled in her ear, urgent and sharp. "Makhtoom, a crowd is coming our way and its heading in your direction." Alisha veered around the corner and stared. "Go," she roared. "I'll meet you in the street opposite the fruit market. Pick me up from there."

Alisha changed course, her boots pounding against the uneven cobblestones. She'd hardly taken a few steps, when she saw one of Al-Jabari's guards rushing behind her into the street. *He's going to spot me.* Just as Alisha sprinted into the street, the guard roared, "Stop." As she tore across the road, she saw that he'd locked eyes on her. He pulled out a phone and shouted instructions into it. *They have their men everywhere,* she thought desperately. *But they don't know my face... not yet.*

In the distance, Alisha saw Raphael's van zooming away. *Good, at least they're out of here.* She ran through the street, aiming to merge into the busy fruit market that was just up ahead. *Al-Jabari's men couldn't be too far.* She wondered to whom the guard had issued instructions over the phone. She'd just reached the fruit market, heaving deep breaths.

Ben's voice came frantically over the microphone, "Makhtoom, we've spotted a sniper in the building behind you. He's a local member from Al-Jabari's gang." Alisha gasped and gazed up to see the sniper aiming the rifle at her. She sprinted in the crowded streets, beads of sweat dripping down her tanned neck. Alisha glanced behind in fear, knowing she was right in his crosshairs. *He had her this time.*

The sniper took a deep breath and calmed his mind. *Snipers were just like photographers,* he mused quizzically. *Both shoot people in such different ways.* As he fingered the trigger, he steadied his heartbeat and pulse.

Alisha had taken refuge behind an enormous basket of oranges. Barely breathing, the sniper watched her. The ripple of her black dress was just visible from his glassy scope. He was amused. He could wait all day. The tall figure in black finally stepped out from behind the fruit basket, hurrying away. The crowd seemed to thin out for a split moment. *I've got her now.* And he pulled the trigger.

His target fell like a cast out mannequin, blood spilling on the footpath. A little girl screamed, and the crowd's attention was rivetted on the fallen figure. A man barrelled out of nowhere screaming, "*Naziha...*" The sniper froze. *This target was wrong, utterly wrong.* Cursing himself, he watched through his scope again.

Alisha's black dress was still rippling within his sight, but it looked as if someone had hooked it to one of the stalls. And then, the sniper noticed a different tall figure, this time wearing a navy-blue niqab climbing out from the *other* side of the fruit stall. He grabbed his rifle again, but he knew it was too late. With a rear glance that seemed to look straight into his crosshairs, Alisha plunged through the crowd, her feet slipping on the cobbled streets of Palestine.

She ran into the opposite street and spotted Raphael's van. They threw open the door for her. As Alisha raced towards the van, a single gunshot went off. She turned to see the sniper's body fall several floors into the street below. She jumped into the van and a masked man followed her. The man pulled off the precision rifle slung across his back and set it on the floor of the van.

As the van roared away, Ben pulled off the mask. "Was that *you* right now? Did you shoot that sniper?" gasped Alisha. "Yep," said Ben. "So, we got Al-Jabari?" Alisha replied, "Yes, we did." Ben nodded at her. "Good job. By the way, Soumik Chandra has reached India."

* * *

The flight was leaving in five hours.

"Your conflict is never going to end, is it?" asked Alisha softly. They were sitting together at the beach again. Ben gave her a melancholy smile and shook his head sadly, staring at the sand. He spoke, "The way you have your Kashmir, we have our Palestine. It's the same situation. Thousands of Palestinians cross into Israel for work every day. Their GDP increased because of Israel. Not all Palestinians participate in Jihad. All those who work hard and have made something out of their lives actually admire Israel, and we consider them as our brothers. But that is never captured in the media. We don't have a problem with those civilians who do not take up arms against us.

The ones who turn to Jihad for quick money are encouraged by the Hamas. Hamas doesn't allow any good development in Palestine or Gaza. All these years, the Hamas and the Palestinian Authority together could've built so many good things and done so much scientific innovation like Israel did, but waging a war against Israel is a better business for them. They could've collaborated with Israel when we became the start-up capital of the world. They receive a lot of foreign funding for this fight against Israel. Besides, an unstable Middle East is always ultimately profitable to America and Russia.

You know, all the children of the top leaders of the Hamas study in foreign universities and receive plenty of benefits, just like Kashmiri separatist leaders. Their children are never a part of their cause. So, they brainwash other little kids and impressionable youth to conduct terrorist activities against us. The only way ahead is peaceful coexistence through education and a broad mind. But it's so hard," he sighed. "There's been too much bloodshed and bitterness. We humans cannot forgive easily. Well, anyway… Let's not talk about that. I've lost too many in my family because of the Hamas terrorists." He shrugged and stood up.

Ben Shapiro shook hands with Alisha. His blue eyes lit up with warmth and a wide smile crossed his face. He pulled her into a long hug. "If you ever come to Tel Aviv again, give me a call," he chuckled. Alisha laughed, "I think that day is going to come sooner than later. I really loved Tel Aviv. Great beaches."

Ben shook his head, still smiling, "Goa is cooler. I'll get Katriel there sometime." Alisha looked at him for a few moments and said quietly, "Thank you, Raphael. It was a pleasure to work with you. I've learnt so much from you." He hesitated for a moment, his smile softening. "Call me Ben. My real name is Ben Shapiro. You're my friend, not just a colleague. And it was a pleasure to work with you as well, my dear. It was great meeting you. But I'm not going to say, 'I look forward to working with you again.'" Alisha burst out laughing. He sighed, "I really hope we don't need to."

Alisha winked at him, "Never say never, bro. And I have someone that you need to meet back in India; my mentor. Your sparring sessions would be spectacular to watch. Oh, and call me Alisha. My name is Alisha Nair." Ben smirked at her, shaking his head.

He jerked his head towards the city, "Let's go eat. I'm going to take you to the Shuk Ha-Carmel to get you some souvenirs and then to the best hummus and pita joint before you leave Israel."

CHAPTER 11

Somewhere in Zurich, Vivian rolled over in bed, exhaustion etched across her face. Suresh Thandan caressed her chestnut-brown hair as he pulled up his trousers. He had a particular fondness for brunette escorts. The lovemaking had been exhilarating for him. Vivian pouted, her lips curling in practiced dissatisfaction, "You haven't bought me a diamond pendant for ages." Thandan rolled his eyes at her, "Not all diamond jewellers are rich, you know." She snapped, "You're just stingy." Thandan shook his head, "I can't afford to. But I will soon," he added with a smirk.

Vivian sat up in bed, intrigued despite herself. "Really?" Thandan replied, "It will take some time. I've inherited some land from my grandfather. And do you know what we found there?" Vivian shook her head, eyes widening in anticipation. "Rare earth minerals," he whispered dramatically. Vivian frowned in confusion. "Oh, come on," snapped Thandan, irritated by her lack of reaction. "Haven't you heard of thorium? Or uranium?" he persisted. She shrugged, unimpressed. "Why should I know? Can that get me a diamond pendant?"

Thandan looked at her in exasperation and yelled, "It's worth more than diamonds, you idiot. Especially with the price that my buyer offered. Just imagine - I was going to sell that land!" He looked at her with triumph, "I'm going to be a very rich man. Then I'll get you something nice." He lightly stroked her nipple, leaning closer. Thandan prided himself on being something of an expert lover, but little did he know that the girls he hired as escorts often laughed at him behind his back.

Vivian asked flatly, "So, when are you going to become rich?" Thandan chuckled, "The process has already started, darling. I'm going to make a deal very soon." Vivian rolled her eyes and pulled the blanket over herself. She spoke in a bored voice, "Just get me my diamond pendant "Now fuck off, I want to sleep."

She pulled up the blanket and closed her eyes. Thandan got out of the bed, still chuckling merrily, proudly thinking that he had exhausted her. He slammed the door behind him, singing as he went out. Vivian opened her eyes. She crept to the peephole to check if Suresh Thandan had indeed left. Satisfied, she went back to the bed and picked up the phone atop her cabinet. Vivian dialled a secure number and spoke softly, but firmly to a mysterious associate, "I've got what you need."

* * *

Alisha Nair stared almost blankly at the smiling air hostess. "Would you like some coffee, ma'am?" It took her a few moments to process the information. "Oh. No, thank you."

She glanced out of the plane's window as the engines roared beneath her. Her thoughts drifted to her conversation with Radhika Menon just hours ago. She had congratulated her upon the successful mission in Israel. Then, with her usual no-nonsense tone, she told Alisha, "Your tickets are booked for Switzerland. There is… a *certain* meeting that I've arranged between you and Suresh Thandan, the diamond jeweller whose name we got while interrogating Abu Tawil's gunman, Nael, in Istanbul. You will pose as an investor. We're going to cut off Thandan's finances before this deal gets finalised. Thandan is in talks with Swiss banks, and once he transfers the money there through his offshore accounts, we won't be able to get it back so easily. I have contacted my Swiss asset. He's arranging for support during the meeting. You'll meet your team members directly at the meeting. I'm sending you a file on Suresh Thandan's personality. Study his psychology well. This time, you'll be battling his mind."

Four hours later, Alisha sat in a car speeding towards a hotel in Zurich.

* * *

That morning, Alisha dressed with meticulous care. She wore a long, elegant white dress, layering it with a beige coat. She opened her bag and chose a long pearl necklace with matching earrings. Sliding a bracelet– a gift from Raghav– around her dainty wrist, she paused momentarily and then applied a dark red lipstick. For the first time in days, she allowed herself to miss him. *People honeymoon in Switzerland*, she snorted to herself. *And here I am, without my husband.*

Alisha glanced at herself in the mirror.

A young, wealthy woman who radiated an aura of sophisticated elegance stared back at her. She smirked with satisfaction at herself. *I do look like a wealthy investor.* She laid out her set of delicate weapons and tucked them deep inside her coat.

At 1:00 pm, she left the hotel to meet Thandan. The meeting was in an apartment on the outskirts of the city. As the car wove through Zurich's streets, she wondered what would happen and who her team members would be this time. Reaching the location, Alisha took a deep, steadying breath and walked into the room with a confident gait.

Suresh Thandan rose to greet her from behind a thick wooden desk. Standing beside him was another figure; a man already engaged in conversation with Thandan. Radhika Menon had mentioned that she would have help during the meeting. Alisha tensed up, wondering if this stranger before her was capable enough to take on Suresh Thandan. But her greeting died in her throat as the tall man turned to smile at her.

Raghav Nair stood before her.

He took her hand in his with a gentle smile. But as his dark eyes fixed back on Suresh Thandan, they were filled with a cold Machiavellian menace.

* * *

Alisha's mind went blank with shock as she stared at Raghav. He turned her around to Suresh Thandan and said smoothly, "Allow me to introduce you to my wife." *What on earth was happening?*

Alisha realised her jaw was still open. Still dazed, she attempted to smile, which was more of a grimace. "Afternoon, Mrs. Nair. Would you like some tea?" asked Thandan cheerfully. Her throat still too tight to speak, she merely nodded. Eyes wide, she glanced at Raghav with silent, accusatory questions. However, he stared coldly ahead at Thandan, ignoring her entirely.

Alisha couldn't believe her eyes. *What the hell is my husband doing here?* She seethed. Raghav, who had been so busy with running his business back home. She stared at him, as though seeing him in a new light, for the very first time.

Thandan continued, "So, Raghav. Let's continue our earlier discussion. How much is Nair Ventures planning to invest in my diamond mines?" Raghav glanced briefly at Alisha, the look unmistakably warning her to not interrupt him.

Relaxing into the chair, he smiled at Thandan. Alisha noticed that his smile did not reach his cold eyes. "No, I am not," said Raghav softly. Thandan frowned in confusion. "Come now, Nair. We've been talking about this for the past hour." Raghav repeated,

"Nair Ventures will not invest in your diamond mines." Suresh Thandan's frown deepened.

Raghav leant forward and spoke pleasantly, "Forget your diamond mines. Let's talk about your land where you've discovered thorium and uranium. How much did Khaled Mohammed Al-Jabari decide to put into your account?" Suresh Thandan's face paled. "Wh-what?" he stammered.

Raghav continued in a dangerous tone, "I'm actually here on the behalf of your competitor, Ambrosia Corp. Or should I say, your previous investors? That was…" Raghav paused and laid delicate stress on the word, "an *interesting* relationship you had with them once upon a time, Thandan. They found out about your embezzlements, did you know that?" Thandan froze. Raghav leaned forward and whispered, "And they're not very happy that you betrayed their trust." He pulled out a small blue file from his briefcase and set it on the desk. Thandan's eyes lingered fearfully over it. Raghav opened the file and flung a newspaper at Thandan. "Read that."

Thandan's gaze slowly dropped to the headline; *'Hamas leader Khaled Mohammed Al-Jabari found dead in Palestine'*. He gasped, "*Dead?* But-but how?" Raghav snarled, "Dead men tell no tales, Thandan. And neither will you." He threw a photo of Al-Jabari's lifeless body on top of the newspaper. Alisha's eyes widened. *How the hell had he obtained the photo that she'd clicked?*

Raghav's cold smile returned. "You do realise you could be next, Suresh?" He pulled out a set of papers, stapled together and waved them. "Is that why you made this deal? You've been in straight losses for a few years now. Were you afraid that the other diamond sharks will eat you up in the market?"

Suresh Thandan snarled at him, "You've no right to-" But Raghav stood up, towering over him. Alisha watched him, frozen.

A smile of cold amusement spread across Raghav's sharp features. He pulled out a phone and dangled it in front of Thandan. "Ambrosia Corp has rigged your factory with explosives. One word from me, Thandan and you will either be saved, or you'd be in complete debt. So, tell me - *who offered to buy your land, Suresh?*"

A sheen of sweat glistened on Thandan's temple. Squirming with discomfort, he loosened the top of his tightly buttoned shirt. He whispered, "I-I can't-" Raghav began dialling a number. "No," yelled Thandan launching himself across the desk. Raghav shoved him back into his chair and roared, "Who gave you the original offer?"

Thandan panted, "It-it is someone from Mumbai. His name is Manav Zakaria. He owns a furnishing business. The money was to come through Al-Jabari." Raghav nodded. "And you're here in Zurich to deal with the Swiss banks." Thandan slumped in defeat. Raghav sneered, "You should be ashamed. You were making a deal with a Hamas terrorist who financed a bomb blast on your *motherland*, Thandan. The Indian government would throw you to rot in Tihar jail for 20 years straight. And, I wouldn't have come this far, had it not been for your... *friend*." Thandan looked up warily. "What do you mean?"

Raghav closed his eyes. "Your old friend at Ambrosia Corp, Dinesh Mehta. He found out that they were coming after you and he begged me to help you. Dinesh and I go way back. I owed him a favour many years ago. He called in that favour for *you*. I'm only repaying him."

Thandan gaped at Raghav, who threw up his hands and spoke, "We have a conflict of interest here, Thandan. So, I'm going to be the mediator. Ambrosia wants *me* to buy the land that Manav Zakaria wants from you. But I'll buy it at a lower price. And just because I promised Dinesh to help you, I'll offer you a position in

Nair Ventures as a manager in one of my factories. Your diamond business can stay with you. You can try to rebuild your life."

Suresh Thandan looked stricken. He spluttered, "You-you can't do this to me. I'll sue you. I'll do to you what you just did to me. I'll kill you." Raghav said quietly, "You will do no such thing." He pulled out a sheaf of papers, tossed a pen, and continued speaking, "Sign this. My property lawyers will call you tomorrow. I've given you a fair price." Thandan read the papers and looked at Raghav with gritted teeth. "I won't sell my land." Raghav gave him a terrifying smile. He hissed, "Then your dead body will be thrown on the streets to the dogs, Suresh. Just like Khaled Al-Jabari."

Thandan closed his eyes and shuddered violently. Alisha stared at Raghav, thunderstruck. She'd never seen him like this. Raghav stood still and watched Thandan palpitate. She sensed that Raghav perversely enjoyed the man's agony. Thandan finally opened his eyes and spoke after a long time, "Give me that damned pen." He bent over the papers and signed them with trembling hands.

Raghav asked him coldly, "And which shell company was Al-Jabari going to use to route the money to you?" Thandan whispered. "Silverpoint Infra Tech Solutions." Raghav said nothing.

Alisha stared at him blankly, letting all the information wash over her. *I can't process any of this.* Thandan handed the signed papers back to Raghav. "You forgot to return my pen, Suresh," snarled Raghav. Thandan handed him the pen wordlessly. He was shaking. "Thank you," said Raghav softly. "And have a good afternoon. Return to India on the next flight. And do me a favour, don't get a heart attack. I still need you alive to sign some more papers, even if Ambrosia wishes you dead."

Thandan breathed heavily. Raghav spat at him, "Go thank Dinesh Mehta. You owe your life to him. I don't have any mercy for Indian traitors who betray their motherland." Raghav rose, tucked the papers into his briefcase and held out his hand for Alisha. She took it, still staring at his face as he gently pulled her upwards.

"I'll see you at Nair Ventures next week, Thandan." He swept out of the room, pulling Alisha with him.

Alisha chanced a final glance back before the door shut after them. Suresh Thandan was holding his head in his hands, weeping bitterly.

❊ ❊ ❊

Raghav murmured, "We have to lie low for a while." Alisha turned to stare at him. She hadn't uttered a word all this while. Their car zoomed quietly over the roads, lush green trees surrounding them on both sides. "You're angry." smirked Raghav, watching the greenery whip past his window. Alisha said nothing.

"Where are we going?" she finally asked. "Interlaken. I thought it's the best place to stay right now." he replied. "You'll like it." He reached for her hand and smiled at her, but she pulled it away and turned to stare outside instead. Raghav sighed.

Alisha felt a mixture of emotions steadily boiling inside her. Shock and fury at the forefront, with a cascade of others trailing behind. The calm voice of reason tried to tell her that she probably should've already expected this somewhere deep down, but she was just not ready to listen to it yet. *Or maybe, I just don't want to.* She wanted to be angry, she wanted to shake Raghav by the shoulders, and scream at him.

The field operative in her warned her to let this go, but the wife in her could not.

They rode in silence for two hours, all the way to Interlaken. As they rounded a final curve, a beautiful sparkling lake stretched out before them. Alisha could already see the white Swiss Alps adorning the picturesque little town from a distance. They pulled up at their hotel nestled near the base of the Alps.

The moment the car stopped, she flung open the door, and stalked off in a huff. Raghav's voice floated after her, "Where are you going?" She snapped, "For a walk." He hurried after her and handed her 100 Swiss Francs. Raghav said hastily, "Then at least take some money with you." She snarled at him viciously, "I have money." He winced. "Okay," he said meekly, watching her stride down the winding road.

Alisha walked around for a while, fuming, until she found a quaint little coffee shop. It was empty, so she ducked inside and ordered a hot chocolate. *What the hell was Raghav thinking?* She fumed to herself. *What if something had happened to him? How deep was he in this?* She took deep, calming breaths and told herself, *I'm sure he has a perfectly logical explanation for this... After all, he isn't a fool.*

She chose a table with a view of the town and the towering Alps beyond. *This is a nice spot.* She stared at her hands and tried to calm her raging thoughts. She finally sighed and rubbed her eyes with her palms. *I have longed for peace and quiet in my life.* Her eyes flew open as a sudden realisation crept in her mind, *but I already have it.* Right now, her anger towards Raghav was far too much for her to see sense. *But, why am I so angry with him?* She wondered.

Alisha glanced longingly at the white mountains as if beseeching them to answer some of her deepest questions about the sudden surprises in life. But she already knew them deep in her heart. It almost seemed as if Raghav had achieved everything his life. *As for me…* she mused. She could easily retire and let Raghav take the reins. She didn't need to work for money anymore.

Alisha could simply continue to lead the elite lifestyle of a celebrity that she was already living… but deep down, Alisha knew that she wouldn't be happy or fulfilled. *I'm not that sort of a person.* The corners of her mouth twitched upward. *I am happier when I serve my nation and my people. At least that gives me a purpose in life.* She wondered if Raghav felt the same. *But we can't do missions together, it's too dangerous.*

Alisha felt her anger fade slowly into a mix of anxiety and resentment. Anxiety, because Raghav had no tactical experience on the field. She felt bitterly resentful because she was kept in the dark. Even she couldn't understand why she was so angry with him. Especially, when she was away for her last mission. Raghav hadn't been angry. He had been worried sick about her whereabouts, but not angry about the fact that she was an undercover agent. She knew that her misplaced anger was not fair to Raghav. In her world, information was on a need-to-know basis, and she understood that very well.

An old gentleman behind the counter tottered over and set a large, steaming mug of hot chocolate before her. He asked cheerfully, "Rough day, *Fraulein*?" Alisha looked up at him and smiled faintly. "Ah – no." The man beamed at her and said, "I see stress on your face, my dear. It is a beautiful day for you tourists. You should go out with your boyfriend." Alisha shook her head and muttered, "I don't want to."

The man waved a hand dismissively. "I lost my wife a few years ago, *Fraulein*. I still miss her, but this town makes up for it. Life is simple, but you complicate it." Alisha scowled, *I don't complicate it, Raghav does.* He smiled knowingly, "You know, I don't even remember the things my *Frau* and I would fight about." Alisha was silent but then admitted, "But, I'm *really* angry, you know."

The man chuckled, "Think - Your anger won't matter in five years, *Fraulein*." Alisha finished her hot chocolate slowly, lost in thought. When she looked up, she smiled slightly, and murmured, "Thank you, sir." He gave her a toothless grin. She put five Swiss Francs on the table, but the man brushed it away and said, "*Nein, Fraulein*. Only three for you." Alisha looked at him, surprised. He announced, "You go and make up with the boyfriend in the remaining two Francs."

Alisha burst out laughing, "Well, tell me what places I can visit today." He told her of all the beautiful places that Interlaken offered. He smiled and pointed to the Alps, "You see that point? There, *ja*." She squinted at the place he was pointing to. "Old nuclear bunker up there, *Fraulein*. Our whole population could fit inside if there was a war. It was made during World War II." Alisha gawked at it. He jerked his thumb at her "You visit *da, ja*? With the boyfriend." She smiled at him and said, "I will. *Danke schön*."

Alisha left the shop, feeling much better. Her anger had faded. The old gentleman's words rang in her head, *Life is simple, but you complicate it*. On the way, she bought some Swiss chocolate and then spent some time sitting on the grass next to a pool. *It was such a beautiful town*. Alisha sighed. *But I must head back*.

* * *

The door slammed shut and Raghav looked up at her, smiling timidly. Alisha sighed, plonked into the chair, and spoke tersely, "You could've told me."

Raghav tilted his head and merely raised an eyebrow at her sardonically, with an expression that silently seemed to say,

'Really? You're going to say that?' She sighed again and snapped, "Oh, I know."

Raghav ambled over and gently squeezed her shoulders. He spoke gently, "Do you think I didn't *want* to tell you? But *you* of all people should know that orders are orders. It was only on a need-to-know basis. There's a reason why they sent both, you *and* me here."

Alisha merely asked, "Have you communicated everything back to them?" Raghav nodded. "They know. I got everything on record, but that's only for the ears of a certain someone whom I can't name. But I'm going to give the credits for cracking Suresh Thandan to *you*. I'm out of the picture here. My people will inform your superiors. You're actually free for the day, now." Alisha stared at the beautiful day outside in silence. She turned to him and asked, "So, do you want to tell me everything?"

Raghav chuckled, "Not today. But I will tell you everything when we reach home. The agency uses business owners and industrialists whenever they require them, Alisha. I don't think even your immediate superiors know that I'm here with you. I was the best bet for this deal. Have faith, sweetheart." His fingers lingered on the bracelet that he'd gifted her. The light shined across the words *'Dharmo Rakshati Rakshitaha:'* on the bracelet. Raghav glanced outside and said, "We have to go back home tomorrow. We just have today to ourselves. Till then, let's just relax, yeah?"

Alisha sighed, mildly upset that there was no more work for her to be done. Raghav seemed to read her mind and said gently, "For once, let *me* take your burden. They told me that you've done enough. I'm so proud of you. You already have a lot of work to be done back home. So, let's take this day while we're here and enjoy the present." He offered her his hand. She looked at doubtfully for a moment, then took it.

They stepped out, and walked around under the mountains. They trudged up the pathways surrounded by tall pine trees. Alisha finally smiled at Raghav when he pointed to a small inn that sold fondue and chocolate. They stood in the breeze with their arms around each other and gazed at a small, beautiful valley right below them. She laid her head on his shoulder. Again, she couldn't help but wonder, *What if something had happened to Raghav?* Alisha gave an involuntary shudder and Raghav tightened his arms around her. He smiled at her – the kind of genuine smile that brought out a small dimple on his cheek. Alisha watched it affectionately, then leant forward and planted a kiss on it.

When they returned, the hotel staff had laid out chairs for them on the lawn. As the sun set over the Alps, the mountains turned pink by the evening and then blueish silver by midnight. Alisha sighed softly and thought, *we got at least one wonderful day together - in Switzerland, as partners.*

Raghav took Alisha's hand in his. This time, she did not pull away. He spoke quietly, "You need to prepare well, darling. This isn't over yet."

CHAPTER 12

Back in India, Soumik Chandra sat in an interrogation chair, groggily. Radhika Menon stood over him as he raised his head and blinked several times. The room seemed to blur in front of him, as Menon's voice reached his ears. The drug they'd used to knock him out still seemed to have some after-effects. When his focus finally sharpened, he realised that she was watching him keenly. Chandra shook his head and said faintly, "I already told you everything I know, ma'am. Sir, please," he pleaded to Ravi Pathak, who was standing back in the shadows.

Pathak's voice was steady but firm, "We're inclined to believe you, Soumik. But you still collaborated with one of the leaders of the Hamas who wanted to take you to an undisclosed location to work for the Iranians. That very act means betraying your country and organisation, especially when you were working on a nuclear-capable submarine like INS Arihant." Chandra shook his head and whispered frantically, "You don't understand. It wasn't just the Iranians threatening me. Besides honey-trapping me, there were some other people from Qatar who had threatened my family if I didn't comply."

Pathak countered, "And you couldn't come to the police with this information?" Chandra laughed miserably, "The police? Sir, they were reluctant to even file an FIR about the scientists who got murdered. Their autopsy reports were forged, too. But you already know that… don't you? Shouldn't you be investigating them instead of me? Not everyone in the police force is corrupt, but the ones who are paid well by external agencies can make your life hell. How could I know whom to trust? I can't even trust my superiors anymore." He said bitterly. Pathak fell silent but continued to watch him.

Radhika Menon interjected, "We'll arrest them all very soon, Soumik. But are you sure that you didn't sell copies of the classified blueprints to *anyone* abroad?" Chandra shook his head. "Ma'am, I was forced to comply. I couldn't give them anything until the final deals were complete." She asked quietly, "Soumik, are you sure that *only* the Iranians wanted you? How do you even know that they were definitely Iranians in the first place?"

Chandra burst into tears. "I-I don't know anything at this point, ma'am. Looking back, all I can say is that you saved me when you had me brought back to India. They would've killed me later. But... now that I can think about it, I don't think that it was just the Iranians who were involved. There have to be other agencies, too. I never wanted to get involved in all this in the first place."

Pathak handed him a glass of water and exchanged a glance with Menon. A silence of understanding passed between them. Soumik Chandra seemed to be telling the truth. They'd been grilling him for a few days, now. Pathak spoke in a gentler tone this time, "Soumik, we can't release you from our custody just yet. But if you remember anything else... that is, anything other than the information that you've already relayed to us, then you need to tell us right away. Conversations, codewords, nicknames, banks, a string of numbers, or companies... anything that might seem even remotely insignificant." Chandra nodded numbly.

Pathak and Menon then moved into another room. Menon leaned against the wall; her arms crossed. "Speed up with the investigation, Pathak. Keep digging up everything you can on Alisha's input which she got from Suresh Thandan about Silverpoint Infra Tech Solutions and Manav Zakaria. Investigating these entities will point us to the right people behind this. If there are others involved, and I think they are, we need to nab them as soon as possible. I fear that they might've left India already. We've been questioning Director Vasant Prabhu of the DAE as a suspect, but we can't get any leads. So, we're going to have to let him go. Oh, and Alisha should be reaching home anytime now. Give her a day's rest and then put her back on the local investigations."

Pathak nodded. Menon then turned to Trivedi, her team member. She ordered, "By tomorrow, we start cracking down Soumik Chandra's superiors. I want you to investigate any senior member of any nuclear organisation who has had unreported or remotely suspicious links to foreign agencies which are not related to work projects." Trivedi replied, "Yes, ma'am." Menon watched him hurry off to make a few phone calls.

Pathak asked her, "By the way, who was the Swiss asset who helped Alisha crack Suresh Thandan?" Menon shrugged. "He's known by his codename, Dhruv. I only received the need-to-know information required for our investigation. I think he didn't want to give up his assets there." Pathak's brows furrowed with interest, and a keen look came into his eyes.

Menon added quietly, "You should be proud of Alisha. She cracked this case wide open, you know." Pathak's expression softened, "I am, Radhika. I always was. But that doesn't stop me from worrying about her. I'm all she's got." Menon gave him a faint smile and said, "She's got others, too. You should know that by now." She walked away, leaving Pathak pondering over her words.

✳ ✳ ✳

"Jay, do we have anything on Silverpoint Infra Tech Solutions?" Pathak called out from his office. Jay hurried over, shook his head, and said, "Sir, it's definitely a shell company. I've been digging up information on its owners, but it is registered to a man who already died two years ago. They've stolen his identity, and I already got his house checked. I'm trying to find out where they're actually operating from, based on their financials." Pathak nodded and replied, "Find that as fast as you can. I'll request the local IB to conduct a raid when you have the location." Jay hurried away.

Pathak pinched the bridge of his nose and closed his eyes. He needed Alisha back on their current investigation. There was something that he was missing, almost like a final piece to a jigsaw puzzle… but he couldn't quite put his finger on it.

It was getting late. *Alisha must've woken up by now*, Pathak thought as he leaned back in his chair. But Jay's joyful shout jolted him. Pathak looked up expectantly to see Jay tearing into his office. "Sir, I got the location," he said grinning and handed Pathak a note. Pathak's eyes scanned it and the corners of his mouth turned downward. *This isn't what I was expecting.*

He seized the secure line on his desk. "Get me the Kolkata IB office, immediately." He waited for a few minutes and the line reconnected. "This is Assistant Central Intelligence Officer Ravindra Pathak. I'm sending you the location of a possible terrorist hideout in a building. I require your team to arrest all the people on that floor. I will send my team over there to assist you with the investigation by today." He listened to the reply and nodded in approval. "Yes, I'll keep you informed," he replied and slammed down the phone. "Jay, you and Kapil are leaving for Kolkata right now." Jay replied, "Yes, sir. But aren't you coming with us?"

Pathak drummed his fingers on the desk and shook his head slowly. "You look disappointed sir," commented Jay. Pathak shrugged. "I'm still missing something, Jay. I think its best if I stay here instead. Tell Kapil to get ready. You're leading this. I'll get you all the permissions required on paper for Kolkata in a short while." Jay rushed off again.

Pathak leant back in his chair and stared at the ceiling. He wasn't sure if sending Jay and Kapil to Kolkata was even a good idea. Years of experience at the Intelligence Bureau had taught him to trust his instincts. *They're not going to find anything in Kolkata. The real operation is happening from elsewhere.*

Gopal hurried into his office next and handed over a report, saying, "Sir, I dug up everything on Manav Zakaria. He seems... *surprisingly* clean. He even has a family and everything on the surface seems to be fine. But there's something in Zakaria's financials that doesn't quite add up. Here-" he handed over a bank statement marked with some yellow highlights. Pathak pored over it, frowning.

Pathak murmured, "His kids are in relatively good schools, and the profit projections of his furniture business seems to be going *just* okay, although not too great. But his personal financials, on the other hand..." he trailed off. Pathak looked up sharply at Gopal. "Check if Manav Zakaria has a gambling addiction. I think *this* is where he might've been desperate for money. He would obviously conceal this from his family. So, get someone to tail him, check the places he visits, and talk to the staff there." Gopal nodded and ran out of the office.

Pathak's mind raced. *Manav Zakaria, a seeming nobody who has everything going smoothly on the outside. But he's desperate for money, and yet makes an offer to buy Suresh Thandan's property... who the hell was controlling this man?*

He hurried up all the clearances that Jay required and left his office as fast as he could. Pathak realised he needed to see Alisha immediately.

* * *

Ravi Pathak and Alisha Nair stared in silence at their whiteboard, etched with black, green, and red names and arrows, trying to piece the trail together. Pathak knew that he was close to uncovering a very important detail, and yet it was somehow eluding him. A stack of old case files and documents lay spread out in front of them. The room was silent, broken only by Alisha clicking her pen and occasionally scribbling on her notepad. They'd lost track of time.

Alisha gave an imperceptible yawn as she stared at the reports. "Sorry, but this couldn't wait. I know you need rest, considering what you've been through," said Pathak gently, patting the top of her head, "There's something I'm missing here." He handed her the reports on Silverpoint Solutions and Manav Zakaria.

Alisha studied the financial sheets of Silverpoint Solutions, shook her head, and murmured, "I need more details on this, *Kaka*. Give me all the information – I don't think we know all the stakeholders of Silverpoint Solutions right now. I want to know everything; right from what their daily schedule looked like." "I thought you'd say that." Pathak replied, disappointed. "I'm trying to get more information on this, but its proving to be really difficult." Alisha fell into thought. "Did you look at all their possible tie-ups? We can question those companies. Their tie-ups would mostly be with shell companies, but if they aren't, then we'll be closer to solving this." Pathak shook his head ruefully and said, "No tie-ups that I know of. I've sent Jay and Kapil to raid Silverpoint's office in Kolkata. Let's see what they find out." Alisha raised her eyebrows. A pondering silence fell upon them.

Pathak murmured, "I felt like telling Radhika so many times that we should've sent someone else to Istanbul instead of you. But I already knew that you wouldn't have it any other way." Alisha smiled at him slightly, "I had help, you know. If I survived an operation in Kashmir, I felt much better about taking up a relatively lighter one. And you would relate to this." Pathak chuckled, rubbing his palms over his eyes. He asked, "When is Raghav coming back home?" Alisha did not reply but simply grimaced. Pathak did not fail to notice that. "You're upset with him." It wasn't a question. Alisha shrugged and made a face at him. She bent over the reports again, but Pathak watched her keenly. She said rather irritably, "Well, Nair can do whatever he wants. Let's focus on this instead, shall we?" Pathak smirked at her, but he chose not to retort. They continued to study the reports and case files.

Alisha finally slammed the reports shut and said quietly, "You've always trained me to follow my instincts. But for this case, what are *your* instincts?" Pathak answered without a moment's hesitation. "I think that there's a final piece that I'm missing somewhere." He kneaded his forehead and murmured, "And it's right there, but I just can't see it yet." Alisha interrupted him, "Or – you don't have information on it as yet." "Perhaps," muttered Pathak. He sighed, got up, and spoke, "I've got to head back to the bureau, but I'll keep my extra copies here for you to study. If you find anything, call me right away."

Alisha winced and clutched her stomach. Pathak's face softened. "Period cramps?" She sighed and muttered, "It's my second day – always the worst. A complete bloodbath." He replied, "Just go to bed, darling and eat some chocolate. You can think better after you're well-rested."

As Pathak headed out, he called out to her, "And stop being so angry with Raghav. The poor boy deserves a break." Alisha yelled after him, "You don't have a wife, Uncle Ravi." He laughed heartily before he slammed the door, "Yep, you see *that's* why I don't, darling."

* * *

In Kolkata, the IB team stood poised to start the raid. Jay Bhadra whispered, "Everyone ready?" Jay, Kapil, and a small team that comprised of local officers and police from Kolkata's subsidiary IB unit stood outside a flat. The flat was on the topmost floor of an old building. This was the operating point of the shell company, Silverpoint Solutions. Pathak's instructions were clear – arrest everyone inside the room. Kapil had already knocked thrice on the door, but there was no response. Jay commanded after a moment, "Now," and they broke open the door.

Jay's mouth fell open. There were computers set up everywhere – it was clearly a command centre. However, there were only two people inside and they looked up in alarm as Kapil rushed at them. Jay ordered, "Identify yourselves." The two men looked scared. *They're not making any efforts to run*, noted Jay with surprise. He turned around and told the policemen, "Seize this room and its computers. Ensure nobody enters this room. And search the building for any other employees of Silverpoint Solutions." Jay turned around to look at the two men who were now shaking. "You're coming with me. We're taking you into custody." *I'll interrogate them there instead of here*, he decided and escorted them by their arms. He placed a call to Ravi Pathak and spoke, "Sir, I've seized the room and taken two men into custody. I'll call you after I finish interrogating them."

Four hours later, Pathak received a call. He picked up the phone and Jay sounded grim, "Sir, you're not going to believe this." Pathak exhaled, expecting the worst. "Tell me." Jay explained, "The two men apparently had no idea that they'd been working for a shell company." Pathak replied, "This happens more often than people expect."

Jay continued, "They'd just finished wiping the hard drives clean on all computers when we caught them. So, recovering the data will take time. Apparently, they were supposed to be here for just one more day and after that, their stint at Silverpoint was going to finish. There were more people working previously at Silverpoint, but they all mysteriously vanished over the past few weeks. I've got their identities, but I don't think we can catch them all so quickly. So, we're going to be stalled on that.

Also, these employees were paid to protect the identity of their boss, even after they'd left Silverpoint. Their boss is a Chinese woman and they'd seen her only once. She has already left Kolkata and is rumoured to travel somewhere in central India. They don't know her current whereabouts. I have a sketch artist with me right now, sketching her face. I'll send you a fax when it is done. I suggest that we alert as many IB units as possible." Pathak responded, "Well done, Jay. Thanks a lot for this. We got lucky by a day. Send me her sketch as soon as you can. And after you're done, come back here right away. I'm going to need you."

I knew this would happen, thought Pathak as he hung up. He stared blankly at his desk. Pathak suspected that the Chinese woman who operated Silverpoint Solutions knew that this shell company had run its course right after international headlines had screamed about the death of Hamas's leader, Khaled Al-Jabari.

Pathak frowned. *People lie, but financial trails don't.* This was an operation where people didn't even know whom they were working for. He knew that the elusive Chinese woman was one of the key people in this operation. *She's a Chinese MSS operative, alright.* But Pathak wasn't sure that they would find her. He pondered in silence. *We still have two more cards to play.*

✳ ✳ ✳

Manav Zakaria felt his muscles tensing up as Pathak loomed over him. Pathak spoke smoothly, "Cooperate with us, Zakaria. You're a smart business owner, you know how it is. This is the best bargain you'll get from us. But you have to give us a name." Zakaria was trembling. Pathak continued, "We'll even let you keep your business. Or… should I tell your partners and investors of all your dirty secrets? Or, even better," Pathak tilted his head and asked softly, "Should I tell your family about your gambling addiction?" Zakaria's head jerked. "D-Don't. I beg you. Please, don't."

Pathak hissed, his eyes gleaming. "Then, give me the name Zakaria, and I'll let you live. Or else I'll make sure your name is splashed in tomorrow's newspapers." He slammed his hands on Zakaria's armchair and snarled in his face, "*Name. Now.*"

"You-you *can't*. You don't understand. They're part of a powerful corporate and they own the media." Zakaria stammered. "They'll destroy me for even telling you." Pathak raised his eyebrows at him, "Then either way, your life will be destroyed. Either by them or by me. And I'm your safer bet. What did they promise you? That they'll take care of your family? Your addictions?" Zakaria was silent. He raised his eyes at Pathak, beseeching him. "Please."

Pathak stared at him and said unexpectedly, "You have two days. We're keeping you in custody till then. After that, your name goes into the newspaper. The choice is yours, Zakaria."

✳ ✳ ✳

Alisha's eyes snapped open. The world looked oddly sideways. A moment later, she realised that she'd fallen fast asleep at her desk. Blinking rapidly, she rubbed her stiff neck, disoriented. *How long have I been sleeping?* Alisha shook her head, trying to shake off her muddled dreams that involved her being chased in Zurich. Uncle Ravi's face suddenly loomed over her anxiously. "Are you alright? You'd been asleep for a long time."

Alisha straightened up and noticed the reports spread across the desk beneath her. Alisha jerked back, thinking, *At least I have a fresh mind, now.* Pathak, standing beside her, gestured at the papers in front of her, "I thought you'd be tired, so I let you sleep." She rubbed her eyes and asked, "Do you have anything from Jay?" Pathak narrated Jay's investigation and Manav Zakaria's recent interrogation.

He sighed. "So, now we have a Chinese MSS operative on the loose. And although I've given Zakaria two days, he's clearly being blackmailed by that corporate he spoke about. And I can't even torture it out of him. Radhika's going over everything once again, but we really need to find something quickly." Alisha muttered, "I'm sorry I slept." Pathak shook his head and smiled, "My team members need their rest to function better." He headed into the kitchen for a glass of water.

Alisha removed her hand that was resting on the paper. She frowned at a name that seemed vaguely familiar. *Why have I heard of this name before?* It was a tiny detail, almost inconsequential. *LevenPort Insurance.* Her brows furrowed. LevenPort provided insurance to Zakaria's furnishing business. They were a new hire and Zakaria had insisted on signing them.

Alisha shuffled through the files, searching for the financial reports on Silverpoint Infra Tech Solutions. She finally found the report and yanked it out. Her eyes searched for answers, her instincts were suddenly urging her to find out. She stared. *And there it* was, *again. LevenPort Insurance.* Alisha was slightly baffled, but the gnawing feeling in her stomach told her that this was exactly what she needed. She double-checked both reports; of Zakaria's business and Silverpoint Solutions and laid them out side by side to compare. *This can't be a coincidence*, she realised. *Both* had LevenPort insurance in common.

"U-Uncle Ravi? I think I found something," she gasped. Pathak hurried over, his eyes alert. "What is it, darling?" She pointed to both papers and simply said, "LevenPort Insurance," and highlighted her findings with a yellow marker. Pathak bent over the papers, frowning. A few moments later, he stood up straight and said slowly, "So *this* was my missing piece." He pulled out a phone and frantically called Radhika Menon. "LevenPort Insurance," he began without a preamble. "Find everything you can on this. I think we've got something major." Menon retorted, "Alright. Give me half an hour on this, Pathak."

The tension in the room was palpable as Pathak paced and Alisha impatiently tapped her foot. Precisely after half an hour, Pathak's phone rang shrilly. He pounced on the phone and Alisha leaned in close to listen. "Pathak," Menon said urgently, "I need you and Alisha to head to Mumbai right away. LevenPort Insurance is a shell company operating from near the embassies and consulates. It seems that their main branch is in Nevada, United States of America. Go to their office and bring their man in our custody. Do *not* take the team with you. Let's try to avoid any kind of diplomatic interference, just in case. I'm coming to meet you in Mumbai. All the best." Alisha rushed around, gathering her essentials. Pathak replied, "Alright Menon, we're heading there."

* * *

The man called Knight was not expecting any visitors today. In fact, it was a holiday for his employees at LevenPort Insurance, and the persistent knocking at his door irritated him. *Probably a courier,* he thought, ignoring the sound. Leaning back in his chair, Knight was in fact, lost in a sensuous reverie. He closed his eyes and reminisced about his last night.

He'd been to a bar and had taken a girl back to his apartment. Her short pixie haircut had attracted his attention. Their rough passionate lovemaking had gone on for nearly three hours. He could still feel her wetness around his arousal, and he became instantly hard at the memory. He closed his eyes and smiled, as he remembered how her smooth legs had felt on his warm chest when she was on top, riding him hard. She'd seized his shoulders and pulled him up with surprisingly strong strength. They'd been nose-to-nose as she grinded harder and harder against him. Knight gave into a feeling of exhilaration as she climaxed, with her head thrown back into a scream. As she fell back into his bed, he'd climbed on top of her and teased her.

That was particularly fun, he thought smirking. He rolled her over and put a cushion under her stomach. He could still hear her delicious moans ringing in his ears as he entered her. His hands had squeezed her breasts as he thrust harder and harder into her. They had climaxed together, and it was the best sex that he'd had in a while. Knight opened his eyes as reality sunk in and he looked around, disappointed. He heard the persistent knocking on the door but still made no move to open it. *Why did they have to disturb me now, of all times?*

The sounds of knocking became so insistent, that he finally relented. He buzzed them in and strode out, fully prepared to shout at the person coming in. *Who the hell was it?*

He stopped when he saw an elegant woman striding into his office. She assisted an old man by her side who required a walking cane. She spotted him staring at her and hurried over. "Ah, hello," she spoke crisply in a foreign accent. "I'm Aleya Thomas. I was hoping that you could assist us." Knight snapped at her, "You don't have an appointment." She tilted her head slightly and said in a calm voice, "I didn't think I needed one, considering it is an issue of insuring about 1.5 million Euros worth of vintage art." Knight hesitated and glanced at the old man who seemed staring into space. "That's my uncle," said the woman gesturing to the old man.

Knight's cold eyes flickered over her. She had an aura of elegance and vintage charm. She was dressed impeccably, with a long pastel blue coat and brown fur boots. *The bitch seems wealthy, alright.* Her uncle was dressed in a tweed suit and was wearing a beret on his head. There was a turquoise muffler around his neck. "Can we continue this private conversation in your office, sir?" she suggested. Knight asked suspiciously, "Do you have any identification on you?" She raised an eyebrow and handed him a British passport and a sealed envelope.

Normally, Knight wouldn't entertain requests. However, he checked her documents and decided to take them inside. *Let's see what they have.* "Come in," he ushered them into his office. The old man walked with a slight limp. Knight offered them glasses of water and they graciously refused, nodding politely.

The woman leant forward and spoke in a measured voice, "We are from Europe, and now have been living in India for a long time. My uncle here served as one of the board members in Schwell Corporation, one of the oldest British defence companies. In the second world war, his father happened to collect plenty of vintage art. Today, that art is valued at over 5 million Euros. We're in the process of moving some of that art to another country and distribute some of it across our homes in India. So, we're looking for a… *discrete* insurance company which would take care of our needs. Please know that money is no object."

Knight gave her a pleasant smile and replied, "Of course. I specialise in all things discrete. We have a list of clients from very fine establishments here. Let me show you-" He turned to his computer and logged in. He didn't realise that the woman was watching his computer's password key combination. "Here," he turned his computer around to show them the screen. Aleya Thomas asked in a slightly cautious tone, "And are you from India?" Knight replied smoothly, "I'm an Indian, but I mostly live in America. I own LevenPort Insurance and I've been in this business for the past 10 years." Aleya smiled at him, "So we're in good hands." She extended her dainty hand to him, and he grasped it in a firm handshake.

Suddenly, Aleya snapped a pair of steel handcuffs around his wrists. Knight snarled, "What's this?" She seized his collar and spoke authoritatively, "We're detaining you. You will be in the custody of the Indian government for some time." Knight sneered, "And do you have a warrant? On what grounds are you arresting me? I'd like to make a phone call to the American Embassy." The woman merely gave him a gentle smile. "No, you're not."

Knight spat, "You don't have any authority here, you bitch." The old man replied, "Actually, she does." He briefly held up an identity card. "We're from the Intelligence Bureau." Knight fell silent. Aleya dragged him by the arm out of his office. She spoke authoritatively, "Cooperate with us, please." Her uncle tailed them close behind.

As they exited the building and stepped on the footpath, Knight smashed the steel handcuffs into Aleya's face. She reeled back and fell against the wall as blood spurted from her nose. Her uncle seized Knight by the neck. *The bastard has a powerful grip,* Knight realised, as he struggled viciously to get free. Knight aimed a kick into his groin, and just for a *fleeting* second, the man's grip on his neck slackened. With a huge jerk, Knight struggled free and sprinted away as hard as he could.

✳ ✳ ✳

Alisha's world turned black for several moments. Excruciating pain surged through her entire face. She tasted iron and understood that her nose was bleeding. She gasped, trying to blink through the pain and confusion. She squinted and saw Uncle Ravi already sprinting after Knight. *He's heading towards the American Consulate,* she realised with a jolt of panic. Alisha ran after them, but they were far ahead. *Our van is on the other side*, she thought desperately. *There's no way we'll make it in time.* Hands shaking, she pulled out a phone and dialled a number.

"Come over to our side of the street," she yelled into the phone, wiping the blood streaming from her nose onto her sleeve. "He's escaped and is now heading to the American Consulate." She watched from afar as Knight collided into a few people and threw them into Pathak's path, creating chaos.

A few moments later, a dark van sped over and screeched to a halt right beside her. Alisha jumped in and pointed at Pathak chasing Knight down the street. The van roared off and Gopal drove at high speed, swearing at the top of his voice as he weaved in between cars. Knight was just a few meters away from the final turn of the short lane leading up to the Consulate. "We don't know if they would give him Consular immunity. Hurry," screeched Alisha. *If anyone from the Consulate or even our paramilitary security sees what was happening, we're done for.*

Gopal accelerated, and the van came to a halt right in front of Knight, cutting off his path. As Knight skidded to stop himself, Ravi Pathak pounced upon him.

Pathak rammed Knight into the van's side. He seized a fistful of Knight's hair and bashed his head against the metal. Alisha flung open the van door and seized Knight. She threw him on the floor of the van and punched his nose in three swift, successive strikes. Knight's eyes rolled back in his head as he passed out. Pathak closed the door and Gopal sped away. Alisha turned to Pathak and panted, "Just in time." Pathak nodded grimly and examined her nose, "Are you alright?" She nodded, wincing. The bleeding had stopped now, but the area still felt very sore.

Pathak reached down and restrained Knight's feet with a black cord. He straightened up and said, "Let's head straight to interrogation. Menon is waiting for us there."

Alisha leant sideways and closed her eyes for a brief moment. She let the exhaustion wash over her. But she straightened up as she suddenly remembered something. "I'll meet you at the interrogation later. Drop me at this bastard's office for now." Pathak frowned at her. She gave him a faint smile, "I know the password combination of his computer. I'll get everything I can before we start his interrogation." Pathak nodded and said, "I'll send some folks your way later." Alisha dug through Knight's pockets and fished out a small phone. She handed it to Pathak and said quietly, "Now, we at least have a needle in the haystack." Pathak pushed the phone deep inside his pockets and glanced at the man lying unconscious.

Finally, a silver lining, Alisha sighed to herself.

* * *

Half an hour later, Alisha was sitting in Knight's seat at LevenPort Insurance, her fingers flying across the keyboard. She entered Knight's password combination and began copying his data onto a pen drive. As she dug into Knight's files and emails, her brows furrowed. *What was this?*

When she realised what she was staring at, alarm bells went off in her head. Alisha grabbed the nearest phone and called Gopal. Before he could respond, she spoke urgently, "We have enough evidence to incriminate him. Tell Pathak that he had help from some very powerful connections in the American Consulate." Gopal answered, "Thanks. We're proceeding to the interrogation right now."

Alisha hung up and immediately dialled Raghav. "It's me," Alisha said, tucking the phone into her shoulder so that she could work hands-free. "Alisha," Raghav's tone was that of pleasant surprise. "I need you to do something for me, *right now*" she said with urgency. "It's a matter of life and death." Raghav's voice came sharply, "Tell me, what is it?"

After Alisha had finished telling him a certain set of instructions, she asked, "How fast can you do this? I specifically need men who don't get carried away by the scent of blood." Raghav replied, his voice serious. "Let's hope we can pull this one off, darling. But call Uncle Ravi right away."

* * *

Knight's eyelids fluttered open; his gaze fixed on the dark floor. *My hands are tied*, he realised. Somebody had placed him in a wooden chair. Knight shook his head to clear his mind. He then calmly raised his eyes to meet Pathak's brown ones. Knight's lips curled into a faint smile; his demeanor unnervingly composed. Pathak watched him intently. *He's too calm for someone to be interrogated. This man is either very well trained or too confident. Definitely backed by power and money.*

Pathak spoke quietly, "You've committed acts of terrorism and treason against your own country." Knight replied with a slight sneer, "*My* country? It isn't exactly *my country*... And you don't have any evidence to prove anything." Pathak shrugged, "Your finances state otherwise. LevenPort Insurance is a shell company." Knight replied still smiling, "That doesn't mean I betrayed India." Pathak said, "You know Silverpoint Infra Tech Solutions."

Knight merely tilted his head and answered nonchalantly, "That's not a question." Pathak chuckled and then his face turned serious. He said quietly, "Your cockiness isn't going to last too long, you know. Everybody eventually breaks down at some point. It would be in your best interests to co-operate with us. I think you know Manav Zakaria well?" Knight bowed his head but said nothing. Pathak stared at him, still analysing the man.

Overconfident. He plunged ahead with his questions. "Why are you targeting Indian nuclear scientists? How did you get their identities? Who's behind their murders?"

Knight shrugged and replied with a certain malice, "You can't do something without some help from the inside… Maybe *you* need to question your own system first. Oh, also… I have the right to make a phone call." "Really?" smiled Pathak. "And to whom do you want to place a call to?" Knight replied, "The American Embassy in Delhi or the Consulate in Mumbai. And the minute they know that I'm here, they're going to swoop in. You really don't want that kind of humiliation, do you?"

Pathak got up and walked out of the room, his expression unreadable. Knight's eyes followed him as he walked away. The police officers standing around watched Knight with bland expressions.

Pathak carefully closed the door of the interrogation room. He turned to Radhika Menon and asked, "What do you think?" She replied, "He's overconfident and extremely smart. But he's not going to make a mistake very easily, Ravi. We need to break him fast. We need to make him think that someone more powerful than his handlers are threatening him. We need to tap into his fears."

Pathak asked, "What about his personal details?" Menon replied slowly, "We don't know too much about him as of now. However, if he was running to the American Consulate for protection and asking for a phone call, then there's somebody very powerful in there protecting him, Ravi. The last thing we want is a diplomatic disaster, so we need to be very careful with this man. However, they don't know yet that he's in our custody, and they can't pull him out of jail if we put him in there." Pathak reflected for a few moments and then wrenched open the door. He strode inside and sat across Knight.

Pathak began quietly, "Tell me your name." Knight did not reply. He merely stared back at him with a hard expression. Pathak held up the sketch of the Chinese MSS agent and asked, "Do you recognise her? You'd insured Silverpoint Solutions to her. So, you obviously met her. Why don't you tell me *her* name instead of yours?"

Knight's face changed into a sneer, "You shouldn't worry about that. You should probably be worried about a certain phone call right about…" He glanced at his wristwatch and smirked, "*now.*"

And Pathak's phone rang.

* * *

Pathak stared at Knight, rooted to the spot. "What did you do?" he growled, advancing a step towards him. "Why don't you pick that up?" taunted Knight in a whisper, baring his teeth. Pathak's hand plunged into his pocket, retrieving his phone. He wrenched open the door and slammed it shut behind him. "Hello?" he put it on speaker so Menon could listen as well. A frantic voice crackled through, "Sir? Sir, can you hear me? Is this officer Pathak?" Pathak shouted, "Yes, tell me."

The voice spoke, "I'm the driver of Director Sengupta, of the Atomic Minerals Directorate. He's fainted in his car and I'm taking him to the hospital. He was foaming at the mouth, sir. He was continuously asking for you when he fainted. So, I called you immediately." Menon fumed as she stared at the phone and mouthed, "*How?*" Pathak urged, "Where are you? How did this happen?"

The driver fairly yelled over the phone to be heard. His voice was barely audible over the roar of wind, "We were at a tea stall by the highway, sir. We were just returning to Mumbai. Director Sengupta finished his tea and then collapsed. I'll call you again from the hospital, sir." The phone cut off. Radhika Menon pulled out her phone and rushed off, already yelling into it, "I need two security teams *immediately* at…" her voice faded away as she ran down the corridor, with her team member Trivedi in tow.

Pathak watched her leave and then burst into the interrogation room. Knight smirked, "Did you-" but he was cut off. Pathak seized him by the throat and with his other hand, he punched Knight with a revolving fist, straight into his mouth. A howl of pain emerged from Knight, "You can't-" But Pathak punched him again, this time in the stomach. He pulled out a police baton from the nearest police officer and smashed it into Knight's knees. Knight doubled up in pain and spat out blood from his mouth. Pathak growled in a low, deadly voice, "*You bastard. Start talking, now.*" Knight looked up at him, panting in painful gasps.

Eyes now seething with rage, Pathak bared his teeth and raised the baton again, ready to strike. *He doesn't have a high pain tolerance*, he realised. *I need to break him and extract a confession before someone from the American Consulate realises that he's missing.* "I'm waiting," hissed Pathak, "If you didn't understand my previous questions, let me ask you *again*. What is your name?" Knight eyed the baton, fear slowly mounting in his eyes.

Pathak hissed softly, "Tell me right now, or else I'll smash your skull and rearrange your brain. Maybe you can answer correctly after that." When Knight hesitated, Pathak seized his hand. With a sudden, swift motion, he bent Knight's ring finger backwards and broke it with a resounding *snap*. Knight's screams filled the room as he writhed in his chair. Pathak seized him by the hair and whispered, "If I hadn't made myself clear before, do you want me to break more bones so that you'll understand better? Name, *now*." He roared the last word.

"Hassan," panted Knight. Pathak studied him for a moment, then slapped him so hard across the face, that Knight felt his teeth might break. "Real name," snarled Pathak. "F-Faisal," choked Knight. Pathak raised his hand again to strike. "It *is* Faisal," he pleaded. "Faisal Qadri." Pathak gestured to the nearest police officer for a pen and paper. He swung a chair around to face him.

"Here's what we're going to do," said Pathak in a soft, deadly voice. "You're going to tell me everything. And if you don't, then I'm going to ask these police officers to hang you upside down and attach wires to your genitals. And I'm going to give you electric shocks right on your privates. You already know that I can be a very serious man, Faisal."

Knight gasped, "They-they won't let you do this to me. I have powerful connections."

Pathak whispered in an eerie voice, "That phone call I just received was not from your friends. So, let's start with '*they*', shall we, Faisal? Now, who are your connections?" Knight did not reply. Pathak gave him a terribly sadistic smile, "Don't make me get the wires, Faisal." Knight stared at the ground and spoke in a low, almost inaudible voice, "The-the US Consul General, Keith Foster." The room went still.

Pathak's bushy eyebrows shot up and he whispered, "I see. And what did he promise you in return for this service?" Knight started shaking violently and his clothes were drenched in sweat. Pathak asked in a dangerously silky voice, "*What did they promise you, Faisal?*"

When Knight looked up, his eyes had a haunted look of vengeance. He whispered, "Revenge for my brother, Atiq. That was all I wanted right since the day your army killed him back home in Kashmir. My brother died in my arms. They promised me an American passport and a job in their government. A position where I would call the shots against the Indian army and military intelligence. A few months ago, when Israel destroyed

Iran's nuclear plant, Iran wanted revenge. I understood them so well. That was my perfect window of opportunity to set things in motion. I could kill so many birds with one stone."

Knight's eyes looked distant as he continued, "It was incredible… At least three countries were ready to damage India. I had arranged a superb nexus with some help from within. Even the investigation would've pinned the blame on some typical Pakistani ISI operative. And the-the Americans gave financial aid to Iran's terror organisations to-to…" he trailed off and stared at the floor. Pathak gazed at him with a harsh expression as he slowly shook his head at him in disgust. He finished Knight's sentence in his head. *To finish this mission.*

And the entire picture suddenly fell into place. As Pathak realised the truth, he suddenly felt complete. *He had recognised the CIA's handiwork right there…* Pathak closed his eyes as his thoughts worked in overdrive.

He murmured softly, "You *fool.* You never realised what the CIA does when their assets turn into liabilities, did you? They only use you and then throw you away after their work is done." Pathak readied the pen and notepad, and said quietly, "And now, you're going to tell me *everything.* Your handlers, your plans, your financials, your assets… *Every damn thing.* And I *will* know when you're holding back, Faisal. Don't make me electrocute you."

Knight's lip trembled for several moments. A police officer picked up the wires lying on the table, and Knight's shoulders sagged in defeat. Finally broken, he started narrating everything to Pathak.

Pathak watched him with loathing. But as he listened carefully, he was struck at how *well* they'd organised it.

The US deep state was truly a ruthless agency.

✳ ✳ ✳

Radhika Menon rushed through the doors of the ICU with determined urgency. The doctor at the helm snapped, "Ma'am, he needs to rest, he's-" Menon interrupted, her tone unyielding. "I know, but please." She held up her hand. "This concerns national security."

Director Sengupta was barely stirring. They had managed to stabilise him, but he was still critical. Menon urged, "Tell me." He slowly opened his eyes, barely managing to string words together. Faint words emerged from him, "The t-tea… Sh-should'nt have…" Menon asked desperately, "Did you see who did this? What can you remember?" He murmured incomprehensibly, "T-the list. The list… M-my…" His head hit the pillow, drifting in and out of consciousness. The doctor begged, "Ma'am please… You can't get anything out of him right now anyway. We need to start further treatment." Menon stepped back, watching the doctors crowd around the director. She ordered, "Do whatever it takes to keep him alive. *Whatever it takes*. He is the director of the government's Atomic Minerals Directorate, and we need him."

A nurse gently guided Radhika Menon out of the room. Trivedi steered her away from the doctors rushing around. It was almost as if Menon felt an invisible clock ticking around her. She turned to the security team and said, "Don't let any unauthorized personnel inside. They might come back to finish the job." The director's driver stood waiting outside. Menon ordered, "Follow me. You need to tell me everything."

Menon gave a last, stricken look at the unconscious director before she strode out of the door with the driver hurrying after her.

CHAPTER 13

"Sir," Gopal called out to Pathak. "You have to hear this. We have a possible tip-off about the killer." Pathak wheeled around, suddenly alert. Gopal spoke with a sense of disbelief, "Apparently, an international exchange student from the BARC complained to the foreign affairs department about a Middle Eastern student lurking outside the director's house with a knife. So, they assigned a plain-clothes policeman for extra security. He had just reached the tea stall and saw director Sengupta take his glass of tea. That policeman caught a glimpse of the suspect tampering with the director's tea. He informed his superiors, and they connected him to us. That policeman followed our suspect and has just sent me the address." Pathak looked stunned. He said, "Ready our tactical team. I'll inform Radhika Menon right away." A few moments later, Pathak was on the phone with Menon.

She ordered, "Alright, conduct the raid, but I need you at the interrogation. Send Alisha there instead. From my side, I'm sending Trivedi over to lead the security team for the raid. They will reach you soon."

Pathak called Alisha and informed her. He continued hesitantly, "Be careful and don't underestimate this suspect. We don't know who we're dealing with. Be prepared and armed." Alisha replied, "Let's hope all goes well. Get Menon on the conference call." When Menon joined, Alisha added, "I'm sending this suspect straight into your custody. I have Knight's data from LevenPort Insurance, just in case." She hung up the phone, leaving Menon staring at it.

Radhika Menon had a faint smile on her face. *I knew Alisha Nair was the right choice.*

✳ ✳ ✳

Alisha silently watched the security team led by Trivedi. They'd reached the place surprisingly fast. "Go in," she mouthed at Trivedi. *If we hang around for too much time, our suspect will know that something is amiss,* she realised. *This was clearly a highly intelligent suspect we are dealing with.* They had orders to capture this assassin alive.

Trivedi's security team had disappeared into the decrepit structure. She waited with bated breath. Beads of sweat had begun to form on her forehead. *Where was their suspect?* She gazed at the dilapidated building. *Why is there no activity inside so far?* She wondered. Trivedi's security team had positioned themselves at the front and back entrance.

But, as Alisha stared at the construction, a growing feeling of dread gnawed at her. *Assassins cover their tracks very carefully... There must be another way if they hadn't found that suspect as yet.*

She quietly walked around the building and climbed over a small moss-covered wall. She glanced down, realising that she didn't need any effort to tread lightly. The whole ground was anyway covered in moss. She walked ahead and froze, as something tinkled in her mind. *Why did the moss here look different?*

Alisha bent down, examining the ground. She could make out a path where the moss had flattened, as if someone walked here often. Her heart hammered. *So, the assassin had definitely been here.* Placing one foot lightly after another, she traced the path, but it only led to a set of gardening tools propped against a wall. Disappointed, she turned away, but a glassy glint caught her eye.

She pushed away a shovel, a muddy watering can, some other gardening tools, and examined closely. Her mouth fell open in shock. There was a carefully covered window that led directly into a basement. She could've easily missed it, had she not been observing keenly. Alisha's heart raced tenfold. *She had found the assassin's lair.*

A voice in her head warned her not to venture inside alone. *This person has probably murdered several people. They can easily take you out in a hand-to-hand combat.* Alisha straightened up and thought urgently, *I need to get backup here, right away.*

As she turned to walk away, strong hands seized her ankles, pulling her down. She promptly crashed to the ground. The window sill painfully raked her back as she went downward. Her mind flooded with terror as she realised that she was being dragged back into his lair.

A thick arm grabbed her throat in a powerful chokehold. Alisha felt the air vanish from her lungs as she gasped for breath. Her bruised legs flailed around desperately, trying to seek some place to hold on. Alisha realised with panic, *I am going to die.*

She instinctively toughened her throat and stared up into the face of death. "Well, this is a surprise" he hissed malevolently. He was surprised and pleased, as though he'd just found an unexpected innocent victim trapped in his lair.

In the dim light of the basement, a terrifying smile lit up his face and eyes… *Those eyes…* The terrifying blackness in those soul-less eyes seemed to swallow her whole. *He's choking me to death…* Alisha's desperate hands shot up and she jabbed two fingers straight into his eyes. The man screamed and his grip on her throat instantly loosened.

She kicked him back and sprang up to her feet, but he blocked her way to the window. Instead, she turned and fled deeper into the basement and heard his heavy footsteps chasing after her. She realised, *the assassin was caught unawares. That means, I still have a few moments to plan my escape.*

As Alisha vaulted over a chair, she dragged it along with her. She turned to face him even though she couldn't see very well in the dark. Years of training had chiselled her well, but she was still terrified to watch him barrel towards her in the dim room with that predatory smile. She realised with terror, *those poor scientists stood no chance...* As if reading her mind, he taunted, "Can't see very well?" Her hands clamped tightly around the chair.

Every muscle tensed up in her body. When he was barely a foot away from her, she threw the chair as hard as she could into his face. He bellowed in pain, and she charged right past him. *That window is my only hope of escape,* she thought in desperation.

She frantically scrambled out of the window towards the sunlight. The moment she was out of the basement, she shrieked at the top of her voice, "Help me, *help me.*" However, he seized her from behind, lifted her up in the air, and threw her hard on the ground. Dizzying white stars exploded around her in the sunlight. *No, not this time,* she thought with gritted teeth, as determination flooded her mind, as a last resort.

Alisha grasped his hand and snapped his little finger all the way backwards with a sudden, swift movement. He screamed in pain, but still held onto her tightly. She realised that her strength was no match for him. She didn't have to beat the assassin with tactical training. She just needed to stay conscious and alive until someone from the security team heard her.

His fingers wrapped mercilessly around her throat once again, and this time, Alisha knew that she was almost out of tricks. As her eyes widened, her fingers dug into his arms, trying to get as much of his skin under her fingernails.

If I die, she thought, *at least forensics will identify him*. She sucked in whatever breath she could muster and held it there, until everything around her faded. As she went limp, his grip slackened very slightly.

As she passed out, she heard shouts.

* * *

Her eyes opened and Trivedi's face peered anxiously at her. She realised she could breathe again. He shook her roughly by the shoulders and splashed her face with cold water. "Tell me you're awake," he urged. She nodded feebly and sat up slowly, glad that her plan had worked.

The security team had heard her, barelled over the small wall, and launched themselves directly at the assassin. She watched the men beat up the assassin as she still coughed and gasped for a lungful of clear air. Her vision slowly cleared as she regained her composure. She did not stop them beating him up. *Let them have their fun*, thought Alisha venomously. *When they're done, it's my turn*. As she felt better, she stood up, and strode towards them. "Wait," she croaked. "Let me."

Alisha lashed out a powerful kick right into the assassin's face, and felt her foot connect with his jaw. He howled in pain, but she reached down and gripped his head. "Not feeling so smug now, are we?" she snarled at him. She slammed his head repeatedly into the wall with such force, that blood trickled down the side of his face. Drawing back her fist, she punched him so hard, that he went slack. Trivedi panted, "Enough. We still want this bastard alive."

As she gazed at the cherubic face of her brutal attacker, she realised, *this isn't a man... It's a boy*. His features didn't look ethnic, either. Trivedi put a comforting arm around her shoulders.

The security team had pooled around them. Together, they dragged the unconscious boy. Trivedi pointed at a van and they threw him inside. Alisha shook hands with the security personnel around her, as she massaged her throat gently and sipped some cool water.

She glanced past all of them and slowly walked towards the concealed window. *I must investigate this.* She gently lowered herself into the basement. In the dim light, Alisha could make out a well-furnished room. *Not bad at all for a basement.* There was a comfortable armchair kept by the door. Several knives hung from a hook, nailed into the back of the door. There was a small wooden chest of drawers beside a table. A few hastily abandoned assignments still lay on the table. Alisha examined them keenly. *So, the assassin was a student.*

The bed had an unkempt appearance and the whole place looked shabby. She pulled out two large handkerchiefs and carefully tied them around her hands. Alisha pulled on a pair of gloves, strode over to the drawers, and pulled them out one by one. Jeans, shirts, innerwear, condoms… the usual. She pulled out the bottommost drawer and pushed aside a few textbooks. Still nothing.

Unwilling to be defeated, her hand reached into the inner slots of the drawer. "Come on," she growled with her brows furrowed. *It has to be here somewhere.* Her fingers probed around till she felt a tiny knob. *There…* Alisha pushed it and froze when she saw the contents of the hidden drawer.

An array of tiny bottles was neatly lined up in a small plastic case. *Was this poison? Or some drug?* Her eyes moved to the other contents, and she suddenly felt sick. Small snippets of hair were carefully packed in zip lock bags. Tiny white labels with numbers, hand-written in black ink, were stuck on the outer plastic. Her heart hammered uncomfortably. *Why was he collecting the DNA samples of all his victims? Was he ordered to, or was it some sick, perverse satisfaction of taking a small part of your kill back home?*

Alisha turned around to see Trivedi approaching her. She held up a zip lock bag and spoke with a revolted expression, "Get a forensics unit here and have them pull this whole place apart." Trivedi stared at it with disgust. He nodded at her and pulled out his phone to place a call.

She placed the bag carefully and went over to the table. She gathered the boy's study assignments and followed Trivedi out of the basement. Trivedi instructed some of the security officers to guard the area, then jumped into the van where they had captured the boy. As soon as he was inside, the van roared off. Alisha climbed into the second car, and it carefully trailed behind the van.

Alisha pulled out her phone and whispered quiet instructions to Menon. "Is the forensics team on the way here? Prepare yourselves. Keep another room ready," she murmured. "We're coming."

* * *

Pathak felt as though he were reliving a horror movie. The bloodied boy was stirring into consciousness and Pathak was already studying him intently. He watched the boy with a laser-sharp focus, analysing him. He looked at the young, handsome cherubic face, free of wrinkles. *He had such a long life ahead of him...* Pathak thought to himself, *all gone to waste.* There was even a youthful glow on his skin. Had the boy not been suspected of such cold-blooded murder, Pathak would've almost pitied him. Pathak wondered how many layers of brainwashing he would have to peel away this time.

The dark black eyes suddenly snapped open and settled on Pathak's brown ones. And without warning, he launched himself at Pathak, but Pathak swiftly shoved him hard in his chest, and the boy fell back into his chair. Pathak kicked the boy in his chest so hard, that the chair slid back several inches. His head was cast down, but the dark pair of eyes roved over the room, taking in the police officers in the interrogation room. Pathak slipped a hand under his chin, threw his head back and said quietly, "Your name and country." The boy didn't reply.

Pathak whispered, "I know you're not from here. It will take me exactly five minutes to find your identity. And after that, it will take me barely half an hour to track your mother, and send someone like you to her place. You know what they will do to her." His words had clearly struck a nerve. The boy now looked up at him and dark hatred pooled in his eyes. "Behzad Hashemi. I'm from Iran," he spat back. And Pathak realised, *the boy has a soft corner for his mother.*

"So, Hashemi," said Pathak softly. "You assaulted several security officers, and judging by the hair samples from your basement, you've murdered several Indian nuclear scientists. We already have a forensics unit taking your place apart." Hashemi sneered, "Then take your time… I'm not telling you anything, and you're going to have to prove that the hair is definitely from your scientists. Won't that need a few days? You have no proof." Pathak gave a faint nod at the police officers around him. They immediately converged on Hashemi with batons. Pathak stood back and watched as they beat him unrestrainedly on his knees, stomach, back, and chest. After the boy's howls of pain turned feeble, Pathak ordered them to stop. "Would you like to tell me now? Or would you prefer another round of beating, this time on your genitals?"

Hashemi spoke faintly, "Water. Please, w-water…" Pathak smiled and struck him hard across his face with a baton. He levelled his face with Hashemi's and said softly, "Ask for water again and I'll whip your circumcised genitals with my belt." Hashemi began to whimper as two policemen pulled his trousers off. Pathak raised a belt to strike and snarled, "Start speaking, *now*. Don't test my patience."

Hashemi's mouth opened, and Pathak had to strain his ears to listen to the words, "I-I only did s-some of them. I was told th-that the s-scientists were helping Israel." Pathak snapped, "Told by who?" Hashemi did not answer. He merely mumbled, "I work for my-my brotherhood and the regime. And sometimes take up assignments from the ISI… It depends on the money. I was also told that my work would help my country against whatever those Israeli bastards were planning. I just get all my instructions through a dead-drop."

Pathak closed his eyes in frustration. *So, the boy had no idea whom he was actually working for.* Pathak asked him softly, "So you killed only *some* of them? There were other assassins like you, too?" Hashemi nodded, staring at the floor. "Do you regret what you did?" This time, Hashemi shook his head, and it took Pathak all his self-control not to strangulate him on the spot. He took a deep breath to calm himself and then strode over to a table.

He picked up a pen and notepad and threw them into Hashemi's lap. "Here's what you're going to do. You're going to confess everything that you did here. I'm going to give you twenty minutes. All the murders, all your activities… Everything. You will write down *how* you killed *every single victim*. And you're going to sign that confession. Or else, I'm going to *order* someone to pay a visit to your mother back at home. If you finish writing in twenty minutes, then your mother lives."

Hashemi snarled, "But my embassy will-" Pathak cut him off, "Your countdown starts now. The Iranian embassy isn't going to do shit because you're already a liability to them. You're in my hands, now. And if you need any help remembering what you did-" Pathak nodded at the police officers, who this time, drew out their belts and converged on Hashemi. "They'll *help* you remember."

Bruised and bloodied, Hashemi looked back at Pathak and tilted his head slightly. That eerie, cherubic smile was suddenly back on his bloodied face, and he whispered, "Then help me remember. I'm not telling you bastards anything. I'll give you a deal. I'll help you with the other killers in exchange for a reduced jail sentence."

Pathak stared at him intently and suddenly realised *he's been playing us all this while… All the evidence points to him, but he's not going to confess.*

He turned around and strode out of the room.

⁂

Ravi Pathak emerged out of the interrogation room, looking exhausted. He strode straight to a secure line and dialled a number. When a voice answered, Pathak spoke briskly, "Provide plain-clothes security officers and police personnel to the Israeli Embassy in New Delhi and the Israeli Consulate in Mumbai *immediately*. Our officers must guard both places round the clock. Nobody stands down until I give the orders." The voice replied, "Yes, sir."

Pathak turned to glare at the two men sitting bound to their chairs in different rooms and then spoke to Menon who'd been watching the boy from behind a mirror, "We have a confession from Faisal Qadri, also known as Knight. This…" he hesitated to use the word, "young *assassin,* however, wants a deal. His name is Behzad Hashemi, an Iranian student on an expired visa. He's working closely with the ISI network in India. You heard him.

He's a very tough nut to crack. Hashemi will name and identify the other killers, perhaps used in the murders of Jayesh Rao, Dr. Uma Rangarajan, and Lalith Gopalan. But he also wants a reduced jail sentence if we want the killers of the other scientists. Also, Knight – I mean, Faisal made several trips to Iran in the past years, so he might've either met the Iranian Royal guards, or someone from VEVAK, Iran's intelligence wings. Or maybe even leaders of the Hezbollah terror group, who might've supplied this boy. I'm guessing it must be Hezbollah."

Radhika Menon murmured, "Hashemi won't get too much of a bargain here – he's been caught red-handed. I've sent Director Sengupta's poisoned teacup to the labs for trace samples. They'll send the results tomorrow. But for now, go and agree to Hashemi's deal." Pathak looked at her darkly. She continued, "I never said that we have to *keep* our word, Ravi. Agree to the deal for now because we're on a timer here. Deprive Hashemi of sleep for as many days as you can. And *then* torture him. He'll start confessing by then. We need all the information out of him, because he will lead us to some more unexpected anti-India sleeper cells other than the ISI, which use such dead-drop services. We might also be able to use him to expose the Hizb-Ut-Tahrir cells across India and other nations. So, we need him alive for as long as possible.

After we're done with Hashemi, either *we* can finish him off or order his jail inmates to kill him there. We can have it staged as a random fight in jail. We can't deport him, and we can't go to the Iranian embassy, either. With the right proof, Hashemi will be an embarrassment to them. So, we can use him to get a bit of leverage over the Iranians for any deal we might make with them. By the way, good job there Alisha," she nodded at Alisha who was standing next to Pathak, scrutinising both the cuffed criminals.

"Are you feeling okay, now?" she asked. Alisha nodded in response. Pathak gently rubbed her back comfortingly and murmured, "Thank heavens I trained you well. You almost rearranged the boy's pretty face, Alisha." She chuckled, "Well, he nearly killed me first. I couldn't have done it without help. Sometimes, you need a small army to do one simple facial." Menon and Pathak burst out laughing.

Alisha sighed and asked, "Any news of the rogue Chinese MSS agent?" Pathak shook his head ruefully. Alisha frowned at them both and asked slowly, "Did Faisal confess as to *how* he got the identities of the scientists? Or Hashemi?" Pathak frowned. "Faisal said that the American Consulate-" But Alisha cut across him, "No, they still needed someone to sell those identities and monitor the schedule of the scientists. Faisal never told you about the mole on the *inside*, did he?" Alisha stared into the distance and then finished with an emphasis, "That's because even *he* probably never knew who it was. He received the identities *directly* from his handlers." Pathak's eyes widened with realisation.

Menon spoke, "When Sengupta was in the ICU, he was mumbling about a list. I think the director had identified the mole in the organisation, that's why he was poisoned." Pathak said slowly, "So… the phone call that I received in the interrogation room was the one that Faisal *expected* from the American Consulate or the Embassy. During the interrogation, he said the words '*help from within*'. Who would that be?" He trailed into a pondering silence.

Alisha took a moment and said, "What if that person is the mole that Soumik Chandra mentioned? And if Faisal is still desperately holding on to some shred of hope of intervention from the American Embassy, then he won't give up that mole. Or he probably doesn't even *know* who it is. He might've said Manav Zakaria, but we already know that it wasn't him. He didn't confess to anything else, did he?" She turned to Menon and urged, "I think we need to search Director Sengupta's office." Menon shook her head and replied, "No. I already ordered my team to search his office. They didn't find anything there."

A shrewd realisation had already fermented in Pathak's mind. *Help from within... Someone who knew the identities and schedules...* He repeated to himself. *I wonder if my idea would work.* He spoke haltingly, "In that case... we need to search their parent organisation - the Department of Atomic Energy."

Menon said firmly, "No. We've already cleared Director Vasant Prabhu of the DAE from our custody, Ravi. And we've already given him a full clean chit. It's been a lot of trouble for us, and we can't go through all of that again."

Pathak gave her a strange smile, "Not him, Radhika. His *organisation.*"

* * *

Alisha's fingers brushed the sweat away from her forehead as she paused to glance at the blue and white logo of an atom with 'DAE' in block letters above the building named *'Anushakti Bhavan'*. She read the motto of the Department of Atomic Energy. *'Atoms in the service of the nation.'* As her team rushed past her with Ravi Pathak in the lead, an amused smirk crossed her face. *Aren't we all atoms serving our respective nations?*

Alisha stepped inside the cool air-conditioned building and felt the humidity disappear behind her. A mix of scientists, government employees, professors, and students milled about. It was a vast campus, but Pathak strode directly to the office of DAE Director Vasant Prabhu. He paused to have a quick word with his team, and they all fanned out to conduct a search.

Alisha, however followed Pathak inside Director Prabhu's office. The Director's voice was already very agitated when she stepped inside and closed the door. "... I already checked that when I got Radhika Menon's message, Pathak. I've lost enough of my scientists; do you really think that we didn't tighten the security? You people grilled me when you took me into custody, even though I told you I'm innocent. What the hell is going on, Pathak? I was wrong to trust you and your damned people. You knew I was framed."

Pathak spoke quietly but firmly, "Sir, the DAE as a parent institute maintains all the data of everyone who's worked in its subsidiaries, including the department of Rare Earth Minerals, the DRDO, and other nuclear institutes. I need access to all those identities who've worked on all the recent confidential projects." Director Prabhu looked hesitant. "Sorry, Ravi. But I can't afford any more leaks."

Alisha pulled the steel handle of the office door and sighed as she stepped out. There was no point in listening to this conversation. So many people across confidential nuclear projects and sectors had been killed. She felt the sagging weight of guilt in her stomach. Miserable thoughts filled her mind, *it would take a long time for Hashemi or Faisal to confess, even under torture... What if more deaths occur?*

Alisha walked over to a bench and sat on it heavily. *This mission was far from over.* She let her head fall back and closed her eyes. *How?* Pathak's team had checked and re-checked everyone over and over again and had grilled everyone associated with all the cases. *There are so many fish caught in this web, that one can barely pinpoint to just one. It was a massive web that clearly made sense at some point, but the Intelligence Bureau are still piecing the data to fully make sense of it all.* She had spent so many days and nights combing through all possible files and financial trails. Alisha pressed her fingers against her forehead out of frustration.

She went over Director Sengupta's words. *A list.* She wondered what he'd meant by that. *Perhaps a list of targets? Someone who had all the information and provided it to the American Consulate or Embassy... Someone who knew the whereabouts of all scientists, and would meet them every day, even perhaps, on an intimate basis… A secret traitor.*

Directly across the floor, she gazed at the blue and white atomic logo of the DAE. She stared at the picture of the electrons orbiting around the nucleus. *One nucleus, holding so many nucleons together… Just like one person, holding all the information, hiding in plain sight.*

Alisha stood stock still as the truth hit her. *Why hadn't she thought of this before?* The answer was staring her in the face for so long, that she cursed herself for not spotting it earlier. She could almost see it laughing at her, dancing at her utter foolishness. For a moment, Alisha grew enraged with herself.

Cursing herself and feeling incredibly stupid, she barged into Director Prabhu's office and asked him urgently, "Who sent you the papers for approval on all these projects? And who did all the billing? Were your fingerprints required at any point in these projects?" Ravi Pathak wheeled around to face her, and his eyes narrowed. Director Prabhu replied slowly, "All the paperwork passes through my close associates. But my fingerprints… Well, that was passed only through the DAE's administrative secretary."

Alisha could barely spit out the words in her fury, "Come with me, *now.*"

✳ ✳ ✳

In the DAE, Neelam Kumari had just finished her work. She picked up her orange handbag and slung it on the crook of her elbow. She smiled to herself, thinking about how comfortable her new home was going to be. The renovations were going to start next week. She remembered what a palmist had told her three years ago. 'You'll have sudden money, but that would be your downfall.' She almost laughed. *Downfall?*

As Neelam walked towards the office door, she saw a team of people who looked like government officials striding right towards her. She froze. The team was led by a stocky man with bright, hazel brown eyes. *This was the same man outside the director's office the other day*, she realised. A silent swearword escaped her lips. Director Vasant Prabhu was hurrying along with him, his brows knitted together in confusion.

Neelam quickly turned in the opposite direction and walked towards the other exit. Her heart was hammering now, but she told herself calmly, *maybe they're not here for you. They don't know anything. You were careful.* As she quickly walked towards the other exit, a tall woman stood directly in front of her, blocking her way. Neelam realised they were here for her. She stared at the window and swiftly calculated the height. If she jumped, she would surely fall to her death. *They will never get me alive*, she thought triumphantly.

Neelam charged desperately towards the window, preparing to jump. She was hardly a foot away when she felt a firm hand seize her from behind. Neelam struggled, but Alisha locked her in a powerful grip, and pinned her on the floor. A moment later, Ravi Pathak had leapt on top of them, and steel handcuffs clicked around Neelam's wrists. She cried out, but Alisha gave a sharp slap across her face. Pathak's eyes were ablaze with wrath. His twisted face loomed over her as he snarled, "You can die later. For now, we need you alive."

* * *

The Chinese MSS operative, Zheng Qui glanced serenely outside the plane's oval windows. *I love window seats*, she thought smilingly. Her mission against India was over. The flight was home bound for Beijing. *My work here is done.* The plane was already taxiing and was about to hit the runway. She was dreaming of seeing Africa again. Strangely, India and its beautiful culture had left a mark on Zheng in a way that she hadn't expected. Zheng reminded herself again, a little forcefully this time. *Your work here is done. Mission accomplished.*

* * *

Radhika Menon had just finished interrogating a hysteric Neelam Kumari. She had initially held up a façade of hostility, but Menon had broken her within fifteen minutes without even laying a finger on her. Alisha watched keenly, as Neelam Kumari's arrogant façade melted away into hysteric sobs. Neelam confessed that she had supplied Director Vasant Prabhu's fingerprints to be planted at the crime scenes. She was the only person who had a secure access to the personal details of all the victims. Alisha turned to Pathak and murmured, "So many brilliant lives wasted for money. All she wanted was *money?*" She shook her head in stunned disbelief. "And Faisal wanted revenge and *American citizenship?*"

Pathak gave her a grim smile and spoke, "People murder for *way* lesser, Alisha. The people in Kashmir who pelt stones at the Indian army currently charge from Rs. 500 to 5000, and those are just basic figures. Throwing petrol bombs, Molotov cocktails, and organising mass shutdowns costs more. I looked up Faisal Qadri's case… He chose to be blind towards the Jihad happening around him when Kashmir was burning.

I guess the Americans had promised him greater things ahead. Faisal was motivated by revenge and therefore they manipulated him very easily. So many Indians among us are even shallower – they do it just for the money and for a much smaller sum to betray their country. A Jihadi takes less than Rs. 100,000 for a well-orchestrated terror attack and takes less than Rs. 10,000 for a murder. For the CIA, this is not even $1000 in exchange rates.

Unfortunately, many Indians *still* do not understand the clear difference between terror, national security, and religion. National security must *never* be compromised under the excuse of religion. It will take years… even decades to truly unite the people of our country. And they don't take efforts to study India's geopolitical strategies, foreign policies, and international trade benefits.

The CIA paid Neelam Kumari way more to sell all the identities of the people who had worked on those confidential nuclear projects. You see, *she* was their lynchpin. They knew her weaknesses and used them to their advantage. They managed to turn the *one* person who had secure access to all the identities that were crucial for them. Neelam Kumari was their biggest asset, much more than Faisal.

You see, the CIA is excellent at recognising patterns. They have hundreds of researchers and watchdogs working on just pattern recognition. The USA doesn't let other countries take away their main businesses. That's why they wage so many wars in the first place. War is one of the best investment tools for a foreign power to expand. At the end of the day for America, it's just good business. They already suspected about Operation Anushakti through the changes in India's financial deals and trade movements. All you need is a few well-placed birds in the political cabinet who sing about nuclear projects and some in the nuclear organisations. A few lyrics are enough to reveal the whole song. They had all the information through perfectly placed pawns, without going in too deep."

Alisha glanced back at Menon's short frame still towering over Neelam Kumari. She asked, "But what about Kumari's handler in the American Consulate?" Pathak was silent. He finally spoke, "It's up to her," he nodded at Menon. "That department is not in my hands. The moment they know we're on to them, they're going to protect their consul general with iron-clad diplomatic walls and recall him back to America. These guys have diplomatic immunity, and the American government won't waive off their powers.

We can arm-twist them in many different ways through finance and trade, though. At a higher level, the political game is very different. But, knowing Menon… I'm sure she won't let him off. She won't tell that right away, but I'm sure she has something in store for him," he finished with a small smile.

Jay Bhadra hurried up to Pathak and murmured something in his ears. Pathak's eyes widened and he stared at Jay. He asked urgently, "Are you *sure*?" Jay nodded and replied, "I've got at least two confirmations, sir. I think we can take them."

Pathak sprinted to the phone and called up a secure line. He growled, "Put me through to the air traffic control." The voice on the other line spoke, "Sir, you'll have to wait for a few minutes." Pathak roared, "We don't have a few minutes. Put me through, *now*." His nerves jangled with anxiety as his eyes fell upon the tiny hand ticking away on his wristwatch.

A different voice spoke, "This is air traffic control. How may I help you?" Pathak rushed on, "This is officer Ravindra Pathak from the Intelligence Bureau. I need you to ground Cathay Pacific, flight 392 flying from Mumbai to Beijing. The Intelligence Bureau needs to arrest a wanted foreign national on this flight." The voice replied, "Sorry, sir. The flight has already departed."

Pathak fumed and looked at Jay Bhadra's stricken face. He continued determinedly, "But has it left the Indian airspace yet?" The voice replied after a small pause, "No sir." Pathak roared into the phone, "Then ground the damn flight *immediately*, before it leaves the Indian airspace. Turn it back to Mumbai and ensure it lands nowhere else. Don't let *anybody* get off that plane. Get a security team ready on the ground when it lands. This is an issue of national security. *Am I clear?*" The voice replied, "Yes sir, right away."

✳ ✳ ✳

A few hours later, Zheng Qui wiped the sweat off her forehead as she sprinted towards the entrance of the airport. *I should've known something was wrong when that bloody pilot announced that there was a technical issue.*

Zheng's flight had been rerouted back to Mumbai. The moment she was escorted off the plane, Zheng pulled out a seemingly innocent-looking can from her bag and had sprayed a chemical into the eyes of the airport security officers escorting her. *My only way to escape*, she thought, as she knocked down the officers and sprinted away.

However, she knew that the security team would set up barricades for her somewhere else. Within minutes, the whole airport would be on high alert.

Zheng spotted a security officer near an information desk and dove behind a column to hide herself. *How had they found her in the first place?* She wondered, panting. She could hear the shouts of her pursuers getting louder and forced herself to stay calm. The entrance was only a short distance away from her and there were only two policemen in her path. *I could run if I tried quickly now.* She straightened up and had hardly taken a few steps, when a tall woman knocked Zheng down.

Zheng rose in an instant and scrutinized her opponent with dangerously narrowed eyes. She prepared to flee, but the woman blocked her path. Like a snake, Zheng lashed out multiple lethal palm heel strikes at Alisha, but this time, Alisha was better prepared. Ben Shapiro's Mossad training kicked in to her instincts and she blocked Zheng's series of blows. As Zheng changed her style of attack, Alisha got a momentary window of opportunity. She suddenly charged at Zheng like a raging bull.

Alisha grabbed Zheng's head and bashed it on her knee. As Zheng faltered, Alisha landed a powerful kick with her heel straight into her stomach. Zheng finally collapsed and Alisha shouted, "Security, over here."

As Zheng struggled to get back on her feet, security officers pounced on her. She looked around wildly but in all the chaos, the tall woman had already disappeared.

***

As Zheng was hauled in for interrogation, Alisha caught a momentary glimpse of Radhika Menon. Menon's teeth were bared and her eyes danced with menace, as she watched Zheng like a vulture about to devour its prey. Zheng screamed at them viciously, "I have the rights to make a phone call to the Chinese Embassy." Alisha smirked. *Everybody wanted a phone call to their embassies.* Menon quickly pulled out a phone and dialled a number. She simply asked, "Do we give her the permission, sir?" She listened to the voice at the other end for quite some time and then hung up.

Alisha realised that the phone call was with someone very senior in the R&AW. Menon stepped up to Zheng smirking. In a clipped tone she spoke, "You can have your phone call now." Trivedi handed a phone over to her and stepped back again.

Zheng Qui screamed in Chinese into the phone. After the line cut off, she sat frozen and stared ahead with a dead gaze. As Ravi Pathak locked eyes with her, he didn't need a translator to understand what had just happened.

China's MSS had ruthlessly abandoned Zheng Qui.

The waves of the Arabian sea lapped over the rocks of Mumbai's shore, spraying Alisha with salty sea water. Her fingers absently brushed away the tiny stones that had pressed into her legs when she'd sat down. Alisha wrapped her hands around her knees and stared into the horizon. *Another sunset on another mission,* she thought with a sigh of relief. A year ago, she'd killed Jamaal Khan at this very spot in the pouring rain. Her fingers traced the small scar where Jamaal's bullet had grazed her. *Still feels like only yesterday,* she mused.

So, this is what it feels like to work with the Research and Analysis Wing, she reflected. Alisha wondered how it must've been for Raghav. How they'd trained him, where he must've met them, how deep his cover was… She still felt as if she knew everything but nothing. Raghav had sworn to tell her everything when she returned home after this mission was over. She had to return back to her life now. A few parties here and there would make up for their absence. Her mouth curved downwards in irritation. *Appearances still needed to be kept.* In fact, even more so, from now on.

Alisha's thoughts wandered to her father, Prakash Kamat. *He could've done so many more missions had he been alive.* Alisha wondered if the recent victims had truly gotten justice. *All those brilliant scientists…* Justice was truly an amusing poetic idea that humans couldn't really keep up with. People searched for it within a court of *law*, but not a court of *justice*. She chuckled sadly. Her past had always reared itself like a vengeful snake. And every time, it had left a searing pain in her chest, but now she'd been able to tame it. *It was only here that I could reach for justice. Not inside a courtroom.* A tear rolled down her cheek as she thought of her mother and father. *I could still claim it for them... I could-*

"I thought I'd find you here," said a voice right behind her. Ravi Pathak stood there, watching her with a gentle smile. He joined her and sat cross-legged besides her on the rocks. "You can't forget what happened here at Sassoon Docks last year so easily, can you?" he said dryly, taking her hand in his. Alisha nodded slightly.

Pathak spoke softly, "The CIA had been paying a few other agencies to get those blueprints that Soumik Chandra had in his possession." Alisha turned to stare at him. He continued, "They had already paid the Iranians and the Chinese. The ISI would've been involved the moment those blueprints reached Qatar. There were all sorts of intermediaries and mercenaries in this case. In the international black markets, those blueprints would've been sold to the highest bidder. So, it will take some time to arrest all the people involved, but we'll get there soon. You saved everyone from a lot of trouble, you know." They sat there in silence, watching the blue horizon turn into fiery gold.

"I'm tired, Uncle Ravi" said Alisha quietly. She laid her head on his shoulder, and he gently rested his palm on her cheek. "And that's okay, darling. It has been a very long day for the both of us," he murmured. "This world isn't made up of people having endless energy. It is made up of people who don't quit."

He looked at her with pride and spoke quietly, "You're a part of the Research & Analysis Wing, now." Alisha replied with a small frown, "And so are you... sort of," she said thoughtfully. Pathak snorted and replied with a grin, "Nah, I'm happy with my Intelligence Bureau."

The sun finally disappeared over the blue Arabian sea. Together, they watched the fading sunrays steadily turn the sky from golden to orange. "Well," said Pathak with a tone of finality. "I have a lot of paperwork and arrests to do. But first, let's have your favourite chocolate milkshake, shall we?" He stood up and offered her his hand.

In her heart, Alisha knew that her beloved was waiting for her.

She took Uncle Ravi's hand with a smile and replied, "Let's go home instead."

* * *

Raghav Nair was drinking coffee when he heard the door slam shut. He had been musing over his pending business tasks. He was pleased to see that everything functioned well, despite his absence. After all, he was away in Switzerland for hardly a few days. But he knew that such missions were very limited for him. He was a businessman, after all. There was still some unfinished business with a certain silver fox.

Alisha turned to see Raghav hurrying towards her. "Is everything okay?" he asked. She nodded and hugged him. He held her there. When she broke away, his eyes lingered on the bruises on her face and neck. Her throat was red and sore where the assassin, Behzad Hashemi had nearly strangulated her. A menacing look filled his eyes as he silently vowed to himself, *I will take my revenge for this.*

He dabbed some medical ointment on her bruises. "I need some rest," she smiled weakly at him. "I know," he whispered. "But we also need to talk," she insisted. He murmured, "Someday, darling. Not today."

Raghav took her hand and led her to their room. He settled on the bed and pulled her down. As he held Alisha's face in his hands, his eyes reflected tenderness and love. She could see how much he'd missed her. With a painful knot in her stomach, she realised how much she'd missed him, too. He breathed into her neck and planted soft kisses along her jawline. She sighed. They did not know how long they sat there, staring deeply into each other's eyes. Whatever she wanted to talk, it could wait. Her eyes fluttered sleepily.

She was finally home.

TWO WEEKS LATER...

Raghav Nair was distracted by his phone ringing at work. The voice belonged to a certain silver-haired gentleman, codenamed Dhruv. "Thank you, my boy. I believe Nair Ventures has finally acquired Suresh Thandan's land?" Raghav replied, "Yes."

The voice replied, "Good. Build nothing over that land until you get further instructions. There would be an offer made to you from the BARC or the Kaiga Atomic Plant. They would use the minerals for India's upcoming nuclear projects. The state's mining laws would apply in this case." Raghav murmured, "Understood." The voice asked, "And how did your wife take it?"

Raghav chuckled, "Not too well. But she realised that we're all on the same team, after all. I think she already suspected it when I gifted her that bracelet last year. And she hasn't told any of this to her superiors. They don't know anything about my role in Zurich." The voice answered after a slight pause, "Then make sure it stays that way."

The phone clicked off. *So, it was done.* A small smile played around Raghav's mouth for a few minutes before he turned his full attention back to his work.

At the other end of the line, the silver-haired gentleman pulled out a confidential brown file with the name, *Prakash Kamat.* He opened it and stared at the little girl in the photo for a long time.

He nodded to himself musing, *it was about time.*

* * *

In Vishakhapatnam, Soumik Chandra's superior, Jasveer Gujral adjusted his glasses as he glanced up from his clipboard, frowning. There was a special team that had just arrived today at the Vishakhapatnam naval office. He wondered what their purpose was. He hadn't been intimated of anything, but Gujral had felt a certain disquiet when a few members of that team had glanced in his way. He wondered, *was this related to Soumik Chandra? Do they know what I did to him?*

He decided to discreetly remove himself from their prying eyes. After all, he had applied for voluntary retirement after his handlers had instructed him to do so. At noon, Gujral decided to leave the office. *I will escape the country... The moment I'm out of here, it will be difficult for them to get me back.*

Just as he walked to the door towards freedom, he felt a strong hand on his shoulder. A voice spoke pleasantly, "Going somewhere?" Gujral froze. He turned around slowly and locked his gaze with a man with stern brown eyes. "Jasveer Gujral?" he enquired. Gujral did not respond. The man continued, "We're arresting you under the Official Secrets Act for co-operating with the ISI and for coercing your junior scientist, Soumik Chandra to act against his country."

Gujral responded stubbornly, "I didn't do anything." The man tilted his head and smiled faintly, "Are you denying the fact that you honey-trapped Soumik Chandra, and then blackmailed him with photos of him in compromising positions? You also bribed three police officers to assist you in all this." Gujral replied, "I didn't do-" but the man cut him off, "We've already found copies of the photos at your home, Gujral. Save the rest of your denial for the Intelligence Bureau. You're also arrested for the murders of the INS Arihant technicians, Himesh Mathur and Ajay Shah."

The entire office watched open-mouthed in shock, as Ravi Pathak and his IB team dragged a screaming Gujral out of his office and threw him into a police van.

TWO MONTHS LATER…

The American Consul General, Keith Foster glanced in his rear-view mirror as he drove his Ford. He was back in America after a very long time. Strangely, he missed the food in India. He glanced at the small American flag on his dashboard. *I've served my country well*, he thought with pride. He was on his way to join his family on a week-long beach vacation. He had dismissed his security agents when he was finally home. He liked his privacy. Foster was waiting for his final assignment. *Nothing too difficult for the next time,* he smiled to himself. *One last assignment before I finally retire.*

Considering his work at the American Consulate and Embassy in India, he wondered if he would get yet another promotion. His thumbs twiddled the steering wheel as his thoughts drifted. There was no traffic on the road, so he pressed his foot leisurely on the accelerator.

His time in India had taught him so many things. Indians were deeply connected to their roots and culture. Foster wondered if he should've stayed there longer. Then perhaps his humane side would've allowed him to interact more with the wisdom of Hinduism and ultimately find peace within his soul. However, he hadn't allowed that to happen too much. *I can't afford to have emotions for a target country.* Foster was an ex-CIA station chief in a few other countries. *I had clear orders*, he told himself firmly. And he intended to follow them end-to-end. *America first.* He remembered his last meeting with his superior at the CIA office in Langley, Virginia before he'd left for India.

The Deputy chief of the CIA had told him, "We can't allow India to make such massive strides in nuclear research and the nuclear market, Keith. It isn't just about our position or interests getting threatened, or our South Asian allies getting uncomfortable. There's also a billion-dollar international market that depends on such countries buying nuclear material imports and so much other raw material. If India started producing locally, that market and our subsequent stakes would suffer major losses. It isn't just American interests here, you see... Many other European nations would be grateful to us, too. There are too many factors and stakeholders in the nuclear game. You put a stop to this in India and then come back here. I have more plans for you after that."

Foster had asked, "What about India's nuclear scientists?" His superior had simply shrugged and snorted, "What about them? Use our assets there to get rid of them. Pretty sure there'll be other agencies who'd be happy to finish them off anyway. I'll give you some of my contacts; There's an ISI asset of the CIA called Professor Farooqi in one of our universities. He can recruit someone and get some more help, maybe even the MSS through the ISI. In fact, there are other mercenaries or assassins you can use for this mission. He is also covertly a member of the Hizb-Ut-Tahrir organisation. While we're at this, we can even disrupt India and Iran's strategic relationship. Just ensure that the finances are routed through a third country like maybe Qatar.

Don't hesitate, we can't afford to pull the plug on this. It is like killing one bird with many stones. We've trained you for this at the Farm, Keith. This should be a piece of cake compared to Iraq."

And he was right. The plan that Foster had devised was simply ingenious. His deal with the Iranians had gone better than expected. An angry, vengeful Knight had landed in his net, ready to do his bidding. He had a near-perfect assassin in Behzad Hashemi. And he was already out of India at the right time, just after his work was done. Presently, he focused on the road again. He wondered what his life would look like post-retirement. *I'll be a great grandad someday*, he thought smiling.

It was just an hour's drive to the beach. As the car turned along the road, a huge black trailer suddenly cut across him. It swerved around the corner, spilling into his lane. Consul General Foster slammed on the brakes, but the trailer didn't stop.

A final scream of terror ripped from his throat as the heavy trailer smashed sideways into his car. His hands flung up uselessly to shield his face as the trailer smashed into the metallic bonnet, all the way into the front seat. The car was crushed into the wall of rock beside the road.

After several moments, a thickset driver emerged from the trailer and hurried up to the wreckage, trying to catch a glimpse of the front seat. He gasped. It was impossible to extricate the man inside without more help. Yet, the driver struggled to reach Consul General Foster's lifeless hand dangling from the smashed window. *No pulse*, he realised.

Several thousand kilometers away, Radhika Menon's phone rang, and she answered it quickly.

"It's done," said a soft, dangerous voice.

* * *

Ravi Pathak turned the pages of today's newspaper and scanned it for two articles. His eyes paused at a small article tucked away at the bottom on page 5, '*Arrested Iranian student killed in jail.*'

He perused the article and it mentioned that an Iranian student, Behzad Hashemi was killed by jail inmates. He was bludgeoned to death by four men who assaulted him with bricks. However, nothing much was written about Hashemi's life. *One chapter was closed, and many souls were avenged,* thought Pathak as he turned the page with a mixture of sadness and grim satisfaction. He already had a shrewd idea of how this was arranged.

He turned to page 7 and read the second article titled, '*ISI network and 7 sleeper cells busted across the country.*' It was a prominent article and credit was given to the Intelligence Bureau and the Home Ministry. A few people were quoted anonymously, and no names were mentioned from the Intelligence Bureau. Pathak gave a sigh of relief. Radhika Menon had requested him to visit Delhi next week and officially close the investigation and mission from his side. He and Alisha had already finished writing all the mission reports. Pathak neatly arranged them all in a maroon file. He stuck a small label, '*Confidential*' and put the file in his drawer. Pathak was supposed to submit this official copy of the file to Menon in Delhi. He was glad that things were much better between him and Menon, now. He knew that they could trust each other on the next mission. *If there was one*, thought Pathak wryly. He tossed the newspaper aside and closed his eyes as he sank in his chair.

There was a knock on his door and his eyes flew open in annoyance. Jay walked in without a word and took a seat right in front of him. He handed Pathak a report and said, "Sir, there's something you need to know. One of the supposed suicides out of all these victims *was actually* a suicide." Pathak frowned at him. Jay continued, "Dr. Iyer committed suicide. The pressure got to him, you see. From whatever we've gathered so far, this wasn't the work of an assassin."

Jay leant forward and said hesitantly, "Sir, if you could write a letter to these nuclear institutions and request them not to put these scientists under so much pressure... Maybe we would've had one victim less. I spoke to their colleagues and some of them admitted that there's so much hushed politics and infighting within these circles, that it can become a very toxic environment to work."

Pathak surveyed him with a smile, "That's very thoughtful of you, Jay. I will write to Director Vasant Prabhu. I'm meeting him next week for a briefing, anyway. And good work on this entire case. Excellent dedication." Jay beamed at him and hurried off.

Pathak watched him go and relaxed back into his chair. *Yet another battle was over.* He felt worn out and slightly tired. *Goa would be a great place to energise myself... I'll probably take Raghav and Alisha with me.* This mission had taken an emotional toll on him this time. But he knew that there were plenty of other battles waiting for him. The corners of Pathak's mouth turned downwards into a small smirk.

Deep down, he was already looking forward to his next battle.

✳ ✳ ✳

At the R&AW office, Radhika Menon was speaking over the phone, "... yes, take care and we wish her well." After she hung up, she turned to Alisha who was standing in front of her. Menon spoke, "A small crude bomb was found under the car of an Israeli diplomat. His wife was supposed to travel in it." Alisha's eyes widened in alarm. Menon shrugged, "She's fine. They were on alert for any possible attacks in case the Islamic brotherhood decided to harm Israeli diplomats in India. We've already made a few arrests and the interrogations have pointed us to a few more people who were already on our radar. It's been handled, don't worry. The sleeper cells will take some time to cool down anyway. Oh, and you've also received a special thanks from my Mossad counterpart. They also mentioned that Raphael says hi." Alisha laughed.

Menon continued, "It always helps when you have friendly foreign intelligence agencies assisting us. You never know how a friend, or a favour pays you back sometime in the future. Especially when we're surrounded by hostile neighbours. This nexus of the CIA financing mercenaries and sleeper cells in the Middle East and using them to overthrow good or bad regimes for their selfish interests is a very hypocritical move. They push down the progress of other countries and have been doing this for decades. There are good parts of the CIA too, you see. But for us, they're frenemies. As long as we're countering China, we're good for them. But the moment we assert our geopolitical or military position somewhere, the CIA steps right in. They wanted an Iranian mercenary to kill our nuclear and missile technology scientists to compromise India and Iran's good relations. They play a perfect domino effect. The CIA knows exactly how to brew trouble in regions where there could be peace. After all, the business of America is… *business*."

She paused and spoke again, "Well, we stopped more assassinations from taking place and saved our missile technology from going into the wrong hands. I'm glad that we killed a Hamas terrorist who also financed a bomb blast in India. Fortunately, the Israelis were already on the lookout for Abu Tawil. He was becoming a headache for Israel and assassinating Tawil got justice for our bomb blast victims, too. For now, we've given a good setback to the CIA. After all, nobody is truly a friend in this world of geopolitics." Alisha asked curiously, "What kind of setback did we give to the CIA?"

Menon did not respond. She merely gave Alisha a mysterious smile and steered her away. Menon suddenly remembered Eli's words at the party at the Israeli embassy. *It's the same people as last time…* She was so deeply immersed in the investigations, that she'd forgotten the significance of his cryptic words. She now realised, *it's the same people as last time… The last time was when*

Dr. Homi Bhabha was murdered. It was the CIA and the US deep state. Menon understood why Eli couldn't tell her directly. And he was right… She had figured it out shortly later. *I owe a big thanks to Eli,* she realised. *I'll send him a bunch of flowers. But for now…* She turned to Alisha and gave her a rare, true smile.

Menon extended her hand and Alisha grasped it in a firm handshake. Menon's face turned serious as she spoke, "I was right about you. Would you be ready to take up further assignments?" Alisha gave her a wry smile. "You think I'd say no to that? I never got to thank you. I learnt a lot from your training." Menon looked at her evenly. "You're a good asset for us, Alisha. You have great connections in the business and celebrity circles, so I'd like you to showcase yourself there for a while until I need you again."

Alisha wondered, *Should I tell her about Raghav?* Sharp as she was, Menon asked her, "Is there something you'd like to tell me?" Alisha hesitated and the moment passed. "No," she replied. Menon asked with a smile, "I'm not as bad as Ravi told you in the beginning, am I?" Menon suddenly looked like a proud teacher gazing at a student who'd scored full marks in their Maths exam. Alisha laughed, "Not at all."

Menon smirked at her, "Well, be there when I need you the next time. The Prime Minister, Defence Minister Surya, and the National Security Advisor have requested me to convey their thanks to you. You might just be invited to a closed-door dinner at Raisina Hill. See you around, Alisha." She clasped Alisha's hand once more and then strode away. Alisha watched her for a while before she felt a tap on her shoulder. She turned to look at Menon's team member, Trivedi. "It was nice to meet you Nair," he said, smiling at her. Alisha bowed her head at him. He showed her the file on this mission and continued, "I have to stow this away in the archives. Would you like to come with me?" She nodded. He said quietly, "Follow me. I'd like to show you something."

They walked down several floors underground. She followed Trivedi down a long corridor. He pulled the door open to a room and quickly ushered her inside. She stared around in the dark. It was a large room and she could breathe the dust in it. Rows of tall steel grey cabinets were lined up over the entire room. Trivedi turned on a dim light and turned to her. He spoke softly, "You remember I told you that your father worked here once? I found something that I thought you'd like." Alisha felt her muscles tensing up.

Trivedi pointed to a small desk. Heart pounding, she walked over to it slowly. A brown file labelled '*Confidential*' was kept on top of the desk. She opened it with trembling fingers. Alisha glimpsed the name printed on the very top of the first page. *Prakash Kamat.*

Trivedi reached over and gently snapped it shut. Startled, Alisha looked at him with confusion. He spoke delicately, "You can have this file *if* Nair Ventures is ready to be an investor in my firm." "What?" said Alisha blankly.

Trivedi gave her a strange smile and said, "A few friends and I are venturing into a start-up which is based overseas. We are making a foray into pharmaceutical software, and I have an offer to head the branch in Delhi. But we need investors for this, and I want Nair Ventures as our main investor." Alisha stared at him in shock. *I can't believe this.*

Anger bristled in her voice as she spoke, "And does Radhika Menon know about this?" Trivedi replied smoothly, "Of course she doesn't. But considering what's at stake here, you won't report me to her, either. Heading this start-up is what I plan to do after my retirement, Nair." Alisha spat at him, "This is blackmail. Government security employees can start their own businesses after taking the right permissions from their superiors." Trivedi said flatly, "It's a take-it or leave-it offer, Nair. You have nothing to lose. In fact, you'll get good returns in the long term. I assure you, that file is perfectly legitimate. I'm sure you would've wanted to solve your father's death in that bomb blast case for years. You have five minutes to decide."

Alisha's mind reeled. She glanced at the file lying just within reach, inches away from her. *If only I could take it with me. I waited for this for so many years.* Her conscience conflicted with her thoughts. *This isn't the right way.* But a small voice spoke in her head, *and was it right when your parents were snatched away from you? Did they get any justice after all these years, when you know that the system is rigged against them?* Her conscience argued with her mind again. *It doesn't matter.*

The small voice spoke firmly this time. *Alisha, you're a part of an organisation that breaks international laws all the time. Then why can't you do this for yourself? This is only a small sum of money in exchange for justice for your parents.* She stood there in silent contemplation. *If you turn your back on this, you will lose this forever.*

Alisha turned around slowly to face Trivedi. She spoke, "Not Nair Ventures. Only me - I'll be your investor." He replied, "No, I want Nair Ventures." She snapped, "You'll get your money, it doesn't matter who your investor is. You have my word. I'm well known in the business circles anyway." Trivedi stared at her for several moments and then said, "Fine. We have a deal, then." He nodded at the file and murmured, "I'll leave you to it." He hurried out of the room, leaving a shaken Alisha inside.

* * *

Alisha stared at the brown file lying on the desk in front of her. She took a deep breath, trying to stem the flood of emotions and memories rising within her. She didn't know what to expect after she was going to open it. *Or maybe I shouldn't*, a small voice of doubt drifted in her mind. *Why disturb the peace of today?* She didn't know how long she sat there, simply staring at the file, her heart pounding.

After what seemed like ages, she reached out a trembling hand and opened the file. *Prakash Kamat, Research & Analysis Wing, India.* Alisha gazed at the name printed in black on the first report. Tears brimmed into her beautiful, dark eyes. She turned over the pages, now staring at his mission reports. *He had written them so well,* she thought admiringly. Her fingers lingered longingly over the places that he'd photographed. *I could've visited all these with him... With both of them.*

As Alisha flipped to the very last page, her mouth fell open. It was a photo taken several years ago. It had slightly faded now over the years, but the faces were clear. She remembered the day it was taken. Her mother and father were sitting on a bench. Little Alisha was standing between them, giggling at something that her father was pointing at.

A cold shiver went down her spine as her shocked eyes saw the dark red circle around her little face. A small 'X' had been marked at the top of the photograph. *So, I was the target,* she realised numbly. Someone had already marked their family a long time before it happened. *But then, why was this photograph kept inside Prakash Kamat's file?*

It was almost as if somebody wanted her to find this file, as if someone from the great beyond was gently nudging her to solve this case. Trivedi seemed only like a conduit. Alisha raised her eyes up towards the heavens, as a tear gently rolled down her cheek. *If only I could know who it was and what happened all those years ago...*

And unknown to her, the mysterious silver-haired gentleman codenamed Dhruv watched Alisha read the file from a dark shadow in the room. He eyes flicked briefly to his wristwatch – he could access this secure room only for some time and couldn't afford to be discovered.

He gave a small smile of satisfaction when she finished reading it. *My wheels of motion were now set for her.*

And the silver-haired gentleman wondered shrewdly… *Would Alisha Nair take my bait?*

REFERENCES

1. Officers from the Research and Analysis Wing of India (R&AW), Delhi.

2. Officers from the Indian Armed Forces and Israeli Defence Forces.

3. Scientists from the Bhabha Atomic Research Centre (BARC), DRDO, and ISRO.

4. Activists who relentlessly pursued the cases of the murders of Indian nuclear scientists.

5. Indian intelligence think-tanks.

6. CIA archives and declassified reports.

7. Declassified files from the US Atomic Energy Commission.

8. The CIA Assassination Manual, declassified in 1997.

ABOUT THE AUTHOR

Asira Lele is the author of 'Veil of Deception', which is the prequel to this book. She writes fact-based-fiction about espionage and counter-terrorism. Her goal of writing this series is to make millennial Indians aware about India's national security and the harsh realities of the life of officers in the intelligence wings. Her writing and research work focuses on intelligence agencies, undercover operations, and geo-political world patterns that create ripple effects in finance, policies, and trade caused by deep state entities.

Indians need to be aware that now, more than ever, they are surrounded by hostile neighbours, deep state entities, as well as treacherous snakes within their own backyard.

In today's 21st century of artificial intelligence, where data is massively misreported, it is also imperative to be aware about world events and connecting the dots of wars, the nexus of banks with politicians, terror organisations, and its subsequent cashflow, its business stakes, and the overthrowing of governments conducted by influential families in the world.

Apart from her job in the software industry, Asira enjoys volunteering as a writer at the International Physics and Science Olympiads. She also loves to travel the world to explore new cultures and countries.